MW00929358

BASED ON A WOO STORY

FIAUNIA WATSON

Copyright © 2012 Author Name

All rights reserved.

ISBN:1536893552
ISBN-13: 978-1536893557

DEDICATION

Sometimes our shadows leave us to lead us from the sky. Inseparable Us: This one is to you, Hakeem "Donut" Brown.

ACKNOWLEDGMENTS

I would like to thank everyone for the support, thanks for giving me the motivation to put my stories to a good use. Thanks for believing in me and giving me all your support throughout the process. Thank you, Torri, Miranda, Nicole, Tarikia, Deanna, Mark, Guy, Issaac, Misty, Renita, Will, Keith, Leilani, Rhonda, Donnie, Malisa "Toothpick," Haley, AJ, Brian, Nasheka, Markel and Dashanti.

Deb, Jackie, Shelia and Tone
To Auntie Q, For strengthening my word game.
Rae- for every push you gave! My sista! My best friend! For never giving up and always having the right things to say.

To Everybody WOO BABY 10 MILLION STRONG

CHAPTER 1: ROCK THE HOUSE

Every summer seemed like the hottest summer ever. By noon everything was in motion and the streets that formed a circle literally came alive. Between these bricks walls is where I mastered the art of being in the midst of my environment but not becoming a product of it. I never had to jump off the porch. I just peeped game from the stoop. Honestly, I just wasn't allowed to go too far. I knew the only way to not get in the way was to stay out the way. I wouldn't say I was sheltered, but my grandmother did not play when it came down to knowing what I was doing. I came from the street lights era, when you already knew what to do when they came on.

Being the nosey little girl that I was, I learned how to see things without actually looking at them. Perception became difficult when I couldn't understand how it seemed as if time had stopped completely one afternoon while walking up Chandler Hill. Apparently there was a raid in our village and a few family members of mine where caught up in the center of the roundup. When I hit the concrete steps of 905 Griffen Drive, my brain was doing triple over time trying to figure out what really was going on. I already knew if I asked my grandmother I would get hit with the proverbial go to statement "*stay in a child's place.*" So I did what I always did, I went to find my grandfather.

It was common knowledge in the family not to tell him anything you didn't want repeated. Matter of fact not to tell him anything, period. He was sitting at the kitchen table smoking his pipe. Paladin Black cherry tobacco filled the air as he stared at the ceiling he took a deep breath. When he exhaled it seemed as if a part of his soul was released. It was in this moment my young hazel eyes saw a sense of defeat in one of the strongest men I knew.

"What happened today Granddaddy, why were all the police over here? Why did they have the school on lockdown?"

He looked me dead in my face and said "*in every game the players do the most work but in the grand scheme of things you never want to become a pawn to those behind the scenes who are benefitting every time you come off the bench"*

I tried to follow him, but to me he was talking in circles.

He took another puff and said "it's so much talent in this community but it gets stifled because of the lack of resources. So these kids chase whatever can offer them that."

He got out his notepad and drew a diagram correlating his theory of how people were sucked in to a pipe dream. Why it was important for me to do my homework and to do well in school. How I had to possess the mentality of the street but at the same time not be of the street. He told me I didn't have a silver spoon but I had a Gold Mind. Before he could take another puff I just blurted out "Granddaddy why did the police come"

He looked at me and said "Crack....I hope they don't try to hang those boys.

It seemed like that last statement drained the energy from my grandfather's whole soul. I watched him get up from the kitchen table, grab his hospital cup, it was filled with ice and Tahitian Treat, then he proceeded to walk down the hallway to his bedroom. I sat there for a minute trying to process the life lesson he had laid before me.

His answer wasn't quite good enough for me so I decided to do some further investigation of my own and walked my way slowly to the living room window. I had watched my grandmother do this several times when she was being nosey. She was a professional at watching from the window without being detected. I cut the lights off, even though it was still daylight and stuck my index finger in the blinds so I could eavesdrop in peace. As I peered through the screen, I saw my grandmother sitting with a few women from the neighborhood whose sons were also caught up in the raid earlier. I couldn't help but to notice that my grandmothers Jerry curl was in desperate need of activator. It looked like somebody put cotton candy on sponge rollers. She had some of the prettiest, toughest hair I had ever seen. She used to swear up and down when she was a teenager her two braids came down to her waist, and her mane was light brown with a hint of strawberry. I think that's how she received the nickname Red. Her hair was beyond thick, and I had her too thank for my mine. Just looking at her hair made me want to run in the kitchen and hide the straightening comb, the blow dryer and anything else that had to do with the scheduled hair combing I had that evening. Blue Magic hair grease was my enemy; I was hoping that the day's events would deter her from remembering that she was supposed to press my hair.

I snapped back to reality when I heard Ms. Rhonda say "All of us probably getting put out over this.

Somewhere beyond my view another voiced chimed in with "Well he wasn't on my lease so they better not try it, cause I'm not for the bullshit. I know for a fact they were not cooking up nothing in my apartment because my stove has not worked since last September."

I knew it had to be Mrs. Rosita because I overheard her husband Mr. Mike complaining to my grandfather that she never cooks or cleans and nothing is wrong with the stove she just won't clean the grease out of it. He came over one day upset about the fact that she drank the last bit of coffee while she was watching the soap operas that she records and rewatches. He was coming to get a pot from my grandfather before he went to his morning job. He worked hard to support their five kids and all she did was talk about the beauty salon she used to own. The ladies complained that she was jealous and would purposely cut their hair so her shop did not last long. Her previous words reentered my mind and I took a deep heavy breath.

I closed the blind and closed my eyes. I saw people get put out before and the sight was not pretty. The maintenance men would just throw your stuff out the window and not care how it landed. I immediately ran to the back, stuffed my Nintendo and camera in my pink book bag and looked around for anything else of importance. I refused to let them catch me slipping. I had to go warn my granddaddy. I went to the back and busted through the door, he jumped up startled and shook his head.

"What is wrong with you girl?"

I took a small breath and whispered "we getting put out so you need to get some of your stuff"

He jumped up and opened the window screen and yelled to the front porch "what is going on Ann?" I heard my grandmother yell back for him to shut the window before be knocked her curtains down again. He mumbled something, got up and headed back down the hallway. I followed behind him slowly. He went on the porch and said "What do you mean we are getting put out?"

Ms. Rhonda jumped up off the stoop and said "I told you. "

My grandmother turned around said "What are you talking about"

My grandfather turned around looked at me and busted out laughing. He pointed his finger at her while saying "seems like somebody misunderstood a conversation they weren't apart of."

She looked me up and down before noticing my book bag.

"Where do you think you're going"

"I don't know but they not about to throw my Nintendo out the window, I'm too close to saving the princess"

The whole porch erupted in laughter. My grandmother shook her head and let it be known "the only princess that's going to need saving is you, if any of my blinds are bent or broken. Now get in there so I can do your hair."

I swear I kicked the hell out of her couch as I went to the bathroom to grab the Blue Magic. I rolled my eyes even harder when the stereo wouldn't come on, I normally liked to drown out the sounds of my hair sizzling.

"Better make it fast or else I'm gonna get pissed

Can't you hear the music's pumpin' hard like I wish"

Salt N Pepa "Push It"

CHAPTER 2: BY ALL MEANS NECESSARY

The following weeks went by slowly as the residents of "The Woo" the nickname Orchard Manor was given, tried to return to normalcy. My grandparents made sure I was mentally occupied. My grandmother bought me all the books from The Babysitters Club series and I gladly read them all. The bookcase in my room was cluttered with a massive collection of literature. I could read a book in a day, and most of the time that is exactly what I did. One sunny humid afternoon I decided to go see who I could talk into "going down into the drain." There was a sprinkler in the center of the housing project that most of us played in when it became too hot.

I got excited when I reached the big tree and saw someone had already cut it on. The housing authority didn't always turn it on so there were a few people in the neighborhood who knew how to get it popping with a wrench. Before I even made it to the sprinkler BJ approached me, with a look on his face that I couldn't decipher. He was a bully low-key, and I usually tried to avoid him. He rubbed his hands together and said "go get some pool passes or don't come over here."

My grandfather had pool passes that he would give out to the kids who picked up trash in the manor. He kept them in his top dresser drawer right beside his tobacco packets. I scrunched my face up and tried to walk away, BJ grabbed my arm slightly twisting it to the point where a sharp pain trickled up my forearm. BJ made me sick, he was a brown skinned, stocky built 14-year-old boy with a major chip on his shoulder. He wasn't attractive to begin with, so his nasty attitude exemplified my disgust times ten. He was always arguing with someone for the pettiest reasons. Some days I had visions of me busting him upside his head with stick, and my best friend Yanni always encouraged me to do it. She couldn't stand him, every time she came around he would ignore her like she wasn't worthy of recognition and she would make slick remarks about how he was a waste of space.

Stepping close to my face he mumbled "go get me some pool passes or I'm going to punch you in the face."

I knew he would do it too because that's just how he was. I looked around and didn't see any of my friends to rescue me, so I nodded my head and went back to my grandparent's apartment.

My granddaddy was sitting in the window in the back bedroom. As soon as I entered the house he yelled for me. Walking down the narrow, mirrored hallway, I tried to keep my cool. He was brushing his hair as he normally did every day. He had some of the prettiest hair I've ever seen it was jet black and super curly. If I had inherited his grade of hair my ponytails would be a lot easier. Instead I was blessed with my grandmothers thick, coarse fast growing mane that was subjected to hot comb pressings on the regular. My grandfather brushed his hair so much you would think he wouldn't have had any curls left. Even though it was natural he would spray my grandmother's activator on it from time to time. This would normally cause an argument because she swore he was the reason the product in the bottle never lasted.

"Come here little girl"
"Yes"

"What did you come flying back around this corner for I thought you were going to get into the sprinkler"

"I need some pool passes"

"For what," he asked, pulling his glasses off his face.

"I just need them"

He looked back out the window. Pointing his finger across the street, he motioned for me to come sit beside him. Before I sat all the way down, he took a deep breath, "Now you know Ernestine was in her back window watching the playground, she told me that BJ was in your face twisting your arms. If you're coming home to get some for him, you got another thing coming. That boy is really scared of his own shadow that's why he only picks with people that are smaller than him. So you go right back to that playground and if he puts his hands on you then you remember how I showed you to stick and move?"

I nodded my head yes.

He did a combination in the air and pointed to the door.

I was convinced he had lost his mind. Was he really sending me back outside to fight a boy. I walked out the door and stopped to tie my shoes.

"Girl your shoes are double tied get over to that playground and tell him if he wants some passes then he needs to pick up trash like everybody else"

Yep he lost his marbles.

. I thought I was going to pass out before I even made it to the playground. I saw it was crowded with more kids now and my stomach did a flip. I turned around and saw my granddaddy standing on the porch lighting his pipe. He gave me the thumbs up and I wonder if he meant the middle finger because that's what it felt like at that moment.

BJ ran over to me, looking half slow "give em here big head!"

Now what did he say that for, I was overly sensitive about my rather large dome because I was I so skinny. I instantly became mad. Looking him dead in the face, I let him know, "if you want some pool passes you need to pick some trash up, that's the only way you're going to get..."

Next thing I know I ended up looking down at the grass. *This fool really pushed me.* I got up preparing to run back to the house. My mind instantly changed when I saw Mrs. Ernestine in the window, my life flashed before my eyes. I knew this moment was a do or die one for me. I could feel it in my soul. I knew she was ready to dial 3043430071 if I hauled my butt back around the corner.

Before I could think of my next move, Ronnie appeared.

"Leave her alone man"

"Nah, she swears she a goody goody two shoes she gets on my nerves, either she going to get me those passes or she can't come over here anymore."

BJ moved closer to me, I wasn't about to let him push me down anymore. I looked at Ronnie, he shrugged his shoulders and said "windmill his ass if you have to but don't run."

Windmill? I was smart enough to know if he landed one blow it was over for me. So I bent down as if I was going to tie to my shoe, and came up with the combination my granddaddy taught me. BJ didn't know what hit him. By the time he realized what happened, I went upside his head a couple more times and I was back on my granddaddy's porch. I sat down, as soon as I looked up I seen a big crowd of kids running behind BJ anticipating a round two.

I stood up when he came up the steps, and put my fist back up.

"You still haven't learned your lesson have you." I heard my grandfather's voice come barreling through the building hallway. He put his pipe out on the railing and got in between us. He looked at the little boy who terrorized half the neighborhood and said "how many of these kids have you gotten into it with?"

BJ mouthed off "I'll go at anybody, word up"

My granddaddy chuckled. "BJ no you won't, you're older than most these kids but yet you stay on the playground messing with them. Why don't you bother the boys your age? You fought a girl today and she won. She's not fighting you again. But she's not going to be scared of you either. You're too hot headed! Trust me keep barking and the wrong person will cool you off. Now if it's the heat that has you agitated go pick up some trash and come back and get a pool pass when you are done."

BJ walked back down the steps. He turned around and stared at me with the look of death. He winked at me and I knew I would have to watch my back. My granddaddy laughed and said "one day I'll teach you how to block BJ!"

He looked at me and pointed to the house. I slowly walked in feeling like he set me up. I flopped down on the couch, before I could say anything, my uncle came in went straight to refrigerator and came back out the kitchen with my last bit of Cookie Crisp cereal.

"That's mine," I said.

He laughed, teasing me, he sang "Bet you want some you can't have none." I ran over and did the same combination I used on BJ on him. Milk was everywhere. The timing couldn't have been worse my grandmother was coming through the door. She couldn't even set her bags down, she was threatening my life, my grandfather was still laughing while she was reaching for her switch in the windowsill. She caught me on the legs a couple of times before I managed to get pass her to the front door. I ran full blast up the street to my mother's apartment. I had simply had enough of the bottom of the hill for the day.

"I never ever ran from the Ku Klux Klan

And I shouldn't have to run from a black man"

Stop The Violence Movement "Self Destruction"

CHAPTER 3: UNFINISHED BUSINESS

I woke up early the next morning, by 8:30 I was dressed and ready to go back to my grandparents' house. Hopefully we could move on past yesterday and her switch was nowhere in sight. But knowing Anne Walters the probability was low. I decided to test the waters, picking up the phone I dialed their number, she answered on the first ring. "Nanny what are you doing I'm about walk down there"

She paused, "you sure are and scrub this wall you got milk on, my arthritis kicked in and I couldn't get it good!"

I rolled my eyes because I knew she couldn't see me. Of course my mouth, my mouth just decided to do its own thing. "You better hope your arthritis calm down before you go to bingo tonight"

"I'm going to work it out right upside your head soon as you walk through that door." She paused, "'matter of fact you stay right where you are because today might be the day you lose your front teeth."

I ignored her threats.

"What time you work today?"

"I go in at ten"

"Ok see you later" I hung up the phone and looked at the clock. Either I was going to walk real slow or I had to find something else to do until she left for work. Scrubbing walls and getting hit upside my head while doing so was not the plan for the day.

The phone rung back.

"You better be here in the next 10 minutes." *Click.*

I would have sworn she was a mind reader but since she could never understand where my aunt was coming from, so that exed that notion out. My aunt Vina was crazy and I hated being left alone with her she was like a Diva in Distress. I knew my grandmother was not a mind reader because she asked my aunt everyday "what goes through your damn head"

I went downstairs to let my mother know that I was going back down the street. Her response was off the wall, she said "let me put some Vaseline on your face." I wanted to pass out. It was already 90 degrees outside and she wanted to shine me up like a special edition penny. I should have stayed in bed. This day was being full of extras and the clock hadn't even struck noon yet.

By the time I reached my grandparents door, I was so irritated that I didn't even notice the hallway was wet. I slid into the apartment and knocked some brass fixtures off my grandmother's rack. She came flying out the closet, with the fly swatter.

"I'm not for your mess today little girl." She pointed to a soapy bucket on the floor and

then pointed to the wall. "Get to it."

I felt like my uncle should be helping since he provoked me. But I knew not to say anything else to her. The whole time I was washing the wall she never closed her mouth. Not once. I don't even think she was breathing, just fussing. By the time she was done I would never waste milk again. Hell I didn't even want to see cereal for the next year.

I finished right on time, my friend Alika who lived upstairs knocked on the door and asked did I want to go to the playground and play kickball. I told her I would go see, it depended on who was playing. If Ace and Ronnie were out there she could forget about it. Last time I played Ronnie threw the ball so hard, it knocked the soul out of my back. I dropped on the concrete and started singing hymns from Shiloh Baptist Church. My other grandmother made sure I went to church on Sunday. I actually enjoyed it, especially Bible Bowl. Trivia was my thing so I was excited whenever we had practice. That particular day when that ball hit my back I recited Psalms 23 with ease. I was convinced that was the only thing that saved me. During my last physical the doctor told me I had a slight curvature in my spine. I was diagnosed with scoliosis. I already knew how I got it, Ronnie and that darn kickball.

Alika and I arrived on Bowman Court just as they were picking teams. Ronnie was one captain and Ace was the other. We both looked at each other and instantly knew we would be spectators. I had two dollars in my pocket I told her I would buy her an icee if she would go get it. It was hot and humid already, and I'm sure the Vaseline was making my skin an open target for the heat. Thanks to my mother I was sitting out there looking like life sized glazed donut.

She came back with the frozen Kool-Aid in a Styrofoam cup that I couldn't get enough of just in time to see ACE roll the ball. He yelled out "Popcorn" just as he rolled the ball fast with extreme force. Jamie saw the ball coming and kicked it with so much power it went flying to the back of the court. Jamie was one of those dudes who was extra talented in everything he did. The kid was extra special; I knew he was going to the league. He was a beast on the basketball court. Jamie was part of the reason half the rims were bent on the court by the creek, dude was dunking in Elementary.

Before Jamie made it to second base an argument ensued in the hallway by the rocks. The housing authority added some big rocks at the back of Bowman Court to add some sort of non projectish look to the manor. We spent most of our time climbing them for a short cut to Lippert Street which we nicknamed "The Circle."

The argument got louder, but nobody moved closer to see what was going on in case we had to run. We all knew the drill, so none of us were alarmed, just cautious. I spotted my little cousin Hasir, walking in the direction of the hallway and yelled for him to hurry up and go home. He took off, I'm sure once he realized I was outside he was heading in the house to play Duck Hunt on my Nintendo. I stood up to make sure he made it all the way down the street safely.

If I was as smart as I thought I was I would have ran after him.

"My hands were all bloody from punching on the concrete."

My Minds Playing Tricks On Me- Ghetto Boys

CHAPTER 4: STRAIGHT OUT THE JUNGLE

The door swung open and Mikey ran out leaking blood, two dudes from New York followed behind him. One was talking cash Ish about being shorted, and the other was adjusting his gold rope chain similar to the one Big Daddy Kane wore.

"Every time we see yo soft scheming ass you going to catch one" the first guy yelled.

He was a brown skinned familiar face I passed from time to time going to the store. He wore Timberland boots every day no matter the temperature was. He looked at the Big Daddy Kane wannabe and blurted out, "you see why I keep my stomp a lame out wheats on 24/8/365 in case I got to get live."

"Yoooo that shit was hard son, you better write that shit down!"

They slapped fives and a ruckus was heard somewhere at the top of the hill. They ran in the direction that Mikey bounced to, and the kickball game resumed. Ronnie took his thumb out of his mouth long enough to kick the ball, it ricocheted off one wall and landed in the green freshly cut grass. Tanika went for it but her long ponytails must have obscured her vision because she bumped into Londa and they both fell down. I thought they would never get up, every time one would try to get up the other would pull her back down, it was pure comedy. Ace was standing in the middle of the court screaming for them to get up. By the time they did actually get up Ronnie had cleared all the bases.

POP! POP! POP!.....POP! POP! POP!

BOOM! BOOM!

POP! POP!

"Talk that rowdy shit now!"

"These our streets don't wear out ya welcome!"

POP! POP!

"Y'all country ma fuckas don't want these problems"

"Fuck y'all pay what y'all owe and y'all can keep the blood inside ya body"

The sound of the drama got closer.

*Man.....*I threw my icee down and went down beside it.

Alika was right beside me, breathing hard. "It's behind this building let's run towards the creek"

She yelled "Creek" and all the kids made a dash for it.

I wasn't allowed nowhere near the creek but they would have to understand today. Once we all got to the creek we watched what could have been a western movie. Mikey and his cousin Steve came back busting at the two dudes who were weaponless. My adolescent blood pressure was on stroke level. I knew that this was only the beginning of long hot summer. The more unfamiliar faces that would appear in our neighborhood the more tensions would rise with situations like this. And if they thought anything different their minds should have been changed today, because one thing I knew those Woo Boys would ride.

POP! POP!

They ran uphill and even though it was presumed safe for us to leave, we decided to play down there where it was much cooler and a lot safer for the time being. We all knew this was about to get ugly. The beef would probably last all day so the kickball game was considered over. The weird thing about it was that none of were really scared. Nobody panicked we just waiting for it to be over, so we could continue our own recreational battle.

Ace stood at one end of a log that stretched across the creek, while we all crossed one at a time. I couldn't swim so I was scared to death. Ace and Ronnie knew my fears so they assured me that I would be good. They always had my back especially at the public pool in North Charleston. They would tell anybody the rules, don't touch her, don't push her in, don't dunk her, don't splash her just leave her be and let her do her own thing in the baby pool. Who knew I would stay in the baby pool until I was 13.

"Called up the homies and I'm asking y'all

Which park are y'all playing basketball."

Today Was A Good Day- Ice Cube

CHAPTER 5: THE LOW END THEORY

The next day at I school I was preparing to pass a note I had just written to my friend Necole when Mrs. Hartwell appeared out of nowhere tapping her ruler on my desk. For the life of me I could not take this woman, she had a major attitude most of the time. And most of the time it was for no reason at all. Don't get me wrong the kids could get hyper occasionally but nothing abnormal. Like why are you a teacher if you act like you don't like kids? Sometimes, I had the feeling that she really couldn't stand to be around us. I wondered how she was with her own children. Did she ever laugh and smile with them? On the brightest days she brought gloom to the classroom. I already knew this wouldn't end well because she had been in a sour mood since the tardy bell rung this morning. When the bell buzzed, on cue she blurted out "no foolishness will be tolerated today save that for your homes." If I didn't think my grandmother and mother would beat the bones out my back. I would have asked her if "she grew up in foolish household or does that only apply to people in the projects."

Tap! Tap!

"Why are you writing notes instead of reading as you were instructed"

Tap!

She tapped my desk again, what for, I don't know, she already had my attention. I guess she wanted to put on a show. She had to be in her late thirties, but she was looking rather stressed here lately. Her pale skin looked dryer than usual and her light brown hair was thin and struggling to have body. I looked up at her.

"I got bored I was..."

Putting her hand up to cut me off midsentence she blurted out with force, "Getting bored was not an option! You do as I say or you will find yourself in detention until school is out."

"I'm finished" I told her pointing at the book.

She gazed at me with piercing eyes. "You are not finished until I say stop reading, understood. You have a whole book to read you don't just stop when you feel like it."

"I'm done"

For her to be a teacher her comprehension skills were not up to par.

"You're right you are totally done! You are finished here in my class! Now be done down to the principal's office you go."

Yo! She just spazzed.

Her face was all read and she was breathing so hard I thought she would whip an inhaler out any minute. Just standing there looking like Professor Pig. I wonder how much trouble I would get in if I asked her was she going to Huff! And Puff! And blow my house down. I knew better than to set myself up like that. My grandparent's did play disrespecting adults even if you were in the wrong. But sometimes my mouth would do its own thing.

I grabbed my stuff off my desk, put it in my book bag and walked towards the door. You couldn't hear a pin drop in the class. Everyone was acting like they were so in to the book now. Well, they very well could have been. It was a really good book. We were reading *Roll of Thunder Hear My Cry.* I teared up in a few parts of the book. Why did I start thinking about this book at this moment? I suddenly got angry and went out the door and slammed it so hard the magnets fell. A few seconds later I heard the door open up.

"Get to the office!"
I passed Yanni in the hallway, I wasn't even in the mood to kick it with her. I'm sure I would see her later. She was probably leaving the principal's office that girl was always in trouble.

I walked down the multi colored hallway and into the office. Flopping down in the chair I mumbled to Mrs. Peters that Mrs. Hartwell worth sent me. A few minutes Mr. Calvin called my name.

I went into office, sat down and stared out the window. I glanced at him and noticed for the first time he reminded of my neighbor Mr. Todd. They had the same low cut with bald spots in the center. Neither were over forty but they both had the demeanor of an older soul. They both probably were losing their hair for the same reason. I'm sure Mr. Todd's kids were driving him crazy, they drove the whole neighborhood crazy, and Mr. Calvin was going bald from dealing with us on a daily basis. Mr. Calvin finally looked up from his paperwork and said "what is this about you refusing to do your assignment but passing notes, did you say you done reading and decline to finish the book read"

"No"

"I've already called your grandmother she is on her way. You could go back out there until she gets here."

I was so glad it was only a few more days left until school was out for the summer. I watched the clock for twenty minutes waiting for my grandmother to hit the office door. I already knew it was a chance I would still get in trouble for writing the note but I knew she was going to get to the bottom of me always getting sent to the office this time.

The door pushed open and Anne Walters stepped in. She was a short, feisty, caramel complected, brown eyed beast. That woman made it happen. She motioned for me to come into the principal's office. Without losing a step she grabbed me up and guided me through the door. I sat down in the same chair and looked at her.

She didn't look at me, she asked Mr. Calvin "is there any way the teacher can come in as well." He told her she would be soon as the school bell rang for dismissal.

"Now what is your version of today's incident."

I looked at him, wondering if I should even waste my breath.

My grandmother reached over and plunked me on the forehead, my mouth started moving on it's own.

"I finished reading and started to pass a note I wrote my friend, she went off and wouldn't even let me explain."

"Explain why you were passing the note?" he asked confused.

"No, that I was done reading that's why I was bored."

The bell rang, he motioned for me to pause and shortly after Mrs. Hartwell appeared in the office as well. She took a seat on the opposite side of my grandmother, then folded her arms in her lap with an attitude. My grandmother took notice and raised her eyebrows at Mr. Calvin.

Mr. Calvin asked her what happened.

She took a deep breath, and said "I instructed the class to read the assigned CHAPTER, I went to the back of the classroom to re-organize the bookshelf for the tenth time this week. It amazes me that these sixth graders aren't taught to pick up after themselves. A little while later I noticed her trying to pass the note. She lied to me and told me she was done after previously stating that she was bored"

I felt like I was on trial, the way she was pointing at me.

My grandmother looked at me and said, "did you lie to her?"

I wanted to roll my eyes so bad. Vina always rolled her eyes. I think one of my eyes rolled on their own but nobody caught it.

"No, she wouldn't let me explain. I tried to tell her that I was bored because I was finished reading the book that's why I wrote the note."

Waving her hand, "Oh please she wasn't finished she was

passing notes. She never opened the book she started writing her note."

If I knew anything I knew her waving her hand like that around my grandmother was not the move to make. My grandmother always told us to keep are hands down when talking or around her before she had a bad reflex that she couldn't be held accountable for.

My grandmother raised her eyelids a second I knew she was aggravated, "how are you so sure she isn't finished? Did you ask her any questions about the book"?

Mr. Calvin looked over at Mrs. Hartwell and waited for her to answer.
"No I didn't ask, why would I? We just started the book 2 days ago there is no way she could be finished."

Looking over at me, sarcastically she asked, "so when you did finish reading your assigned CHAPTER?"
"I finished reading the whole book yesterday"

She smirked and rolled her eyes. "Lies"

"The Devil is lie!" I said.

My grandmother and Mr. Calvin looked at me like I was crazy. I swear I heard him chuckle softy. I always wanted to say that my granny always said that at church.

My grandmother leaned closer to her forcing her to make eye contact. She pointed at me and let her have it. "She can read a book in a day, is this what you had me walk all the way down here for in the heat of the day Mr. Calvin? Because her teacher failed to believe that she could possibly be done with the book. Please tell me I didn't come all the way to this school for that? You mean she wasn't being disrespectful, she didn't slap anybody's child, pull a fire alarm. I'm here because her teacher didn't take the time out to ask any questions to find out if she really read the book. She just assumed that it was impossible and my granddaughter who has been reading since she was three was incapable of completing such a task. Is that why I'm Mr. Calvin?"

The principal began to scratch hair that wasn't on his head.

Mr. Calvin knew better to direct any questions to Mrs. Hartwell at this point or my grandmother so he asked me "what was the main thing that stuck out to you in the book"

I wasn't sure if he realized he threw me the perfect alley oop.

"That people sometimes judge you before they get a chance to know you based off how you look or where you live."

I looked over at my teacher, she was getting redder by the moment. I smirked, and mentally prepared this combination on her.

"What do you mean?" He leaned back in his chair, he was going to leave the lane open for me.

"She's just rude she never uses good morning, all she says is leave the foolishness at your homes, but the fact that she starts the day off so negative is foolish to me."

My grandmother and Mr. Calvin stiffened. I was about to milk this.

"Can I go back to Mrs. Lanes class, she's so nice and helpful?"

"You can't go backwards a grade plus you'll be in junior high next year."

"I can't go forward with her negativity."

My grandmother looked over at my teacher and said "you should get to know you kids a little better, A lot of them are smart because we don't tolerate foolishness at home"

My grandmother motioned for me to get up, she told Mr.

Calvin, "I ought to call a cab home on your expense. I won't make you reach in your pocket today because I'm sure you have hands full here."

Mrs. Hartwell was now the color of Tahitian Treat.

Yeah this album is dedicated to all the teachers that told me

I'd never amount to nothing

"Juicy" Notorious B.I.G.

CHAPTER 6: CHECK YOUR HEAD

I hated getting my hair braided but it took the stress away from having to get it done every day. I had about a hundred small plaits in my head with about six or seven beads in multi colors at the bottom of each one. You couldn't tell me nothing when I had my had my beads in. I would stand in front of the box fan and sing "How will I know" by Whitney Houston until I went hoarse, but today I almost lost one of my main senses by not exercising common sense. In the process of hitting all the right notes, and shaking my head to the beat a rogue braid went haywire and popped me in the eye. I went blind for three minutes, I saw stars, stripes, Hayley's Comet and the light. I just knew in my soul I would get a whipping because my mother would tell me every day to stop swinging my braids before I put my eye out. I could hear her now, "That's exactly what you get for being hard headed now you have to walk around here with one eye, and people are going to say who's that one eyed little girl."

I kicked the couch and flopped down in my grandmother's recliner. I waited patiently for my eye to stop running salty water or just go on and roll right on out my head. In the process of waiting and preparing for my final moments with my vision, my aunt came in the house stared at me.

"What you sitting up in this hot ass house crying for"

In the midst of my agony I had turned the fan off for being an accessory to my pain.

"I'm not crying!" I yelled

"Who you yelling at, take your weird ass outside and play. I'm about to watch tv so you're coming UP out of the living room."

She killed me acting like nobody could watch tv with her and she had to watch it in peace. As pretty as she was, she had the attitude of a wildebeest. She went in the bathroom and I ran over to the television and unplugged the chord in the back then proceeded back out on the porch. The sun instantly dried up the remaining drops of water in my eye, but it was still sensitive to the light. I was just thankful I could still see.

I could hear my aunt Toya in the house fussing about the old television going out, I laughed as I heard her on the phone bothering my grandmother at work about calling ColorTyme to come fix it. My grandmother must have hung up on her because she was now on the porch beside me complaining about how hot it was.

A short while later her friend Niyah joined us on the porch and they began talking about the girl up the street named Jasmine. Apparently Jasmine was saying she was pregnant by somebody's boyfriend and everybody knew but her own boyfriend. And whoever the guy she was supposedly pregnant by wasn't claiming the baby. His girlfriend wanted to fight Jasmine but she wouldn't come outside. So the girl was sitting on the side of Jasmine's building waiting for her slip up. Niyah told Vina, Jasmine was trying to put that baby on anybody, she keeps saying the dude is in jail and it's nobody's business but hers. The girl who was trying to fight her had pulled up in Black Explorer and stayed outside building staring up at Jasmine's window with her big brown eyes. She was awfully bold to come to this neighborhood and pop off. I wondered who her boyfriend was, it had to be somebody who was somebody because she was surely feeling herself the long way.

I almost got caught slipping myself when my grandmother came out nowhere.

"What are you doing sitting out here with them listening to their nonsense. What did I tell you about sitting up under grown folks trying to hear hustle? You and Tonika kill me."

I flew in the house, plugged the television back up and ran in the kitchen to grab a Popsicle out of the deep freezer where I hid them the other day. My grandfather had a habit of passing all of them out and not saving any for me.

My grandmother came in the house, dropped her purse, it hit the couch with a thud, because of the papers and change she kept in it. She walked over to television punch the power button, the television came right on. She changed the channel to make sure it was working. Shaking her head, she went on the front porch pulled my aunt up by her bun and pulled her back into the apartment.

My neck was about to explode trying to contain my laughter.

"Don't you ever bother me at work, about a damn television that works perfectly fine. If you want a better one you buy it."

My aunt stood there changing the channels in a state of confusion.

"It would not come on for me." She turned and looked at me and said "didn't it stay black"

I shrugged my shoulders, "I don't know you told me to take my weird Cussword outside"

If looks could kill I would have been embalmed on the spot.

My grandmother popped her.

"What I tell you about calling her names?" She proceeded to

lecture her about hanging out in the streets all hours of the night, how life wasn't no joke and how short life could be. My aunt was not listening because we could all hear Toya yelling for her to come back out, Jasmine had finally come out of her building. She flew past my grandmother to the door, and we went after her to see what the commotion was about.

My grandmother looked at Toya and a weird look came across her face, she paused before she looked her dead in her face and said "why you looking so skinny lately." I caught a glimpse of my aunts face and it looked like she swallowed a sour patch whole. My grandmother could be rude at times.

Before a stunned Toya could answer, a high pitch wail came cascading down the hill from Jasmine's nemesis.

That girl waited six hours in the hot sun for Jasmine to come out of her building, Jasmine beat the hell out of her, drug her to the sidewalk and went back in the apartment she had resided in since birth like nothing happened.

"Don't call it a comeback....I been here for years" LL COOL J *"Mama Said Knock You Out"*

CHAPTER 7: BUSINESS NEVER PERSONAL

The days passed by filled with sweltering heat, and more and more unfamiliar cars passed through the small circular project. They came for one thing and left as soon as they got it. A large majority of the faces did not look like mine. My grandmother would often tell me that it was too much going on outside, and for me to just stay on the porch. I developed my skills as a professional people watcher in the summer of 89. I saw the cars come and go, some of their faces became regular to me, I knew which part of the project they would go to and about how long they would stay before they made an exit. The people in the cars hardly ever got out, they would stop in front of a building, or a corner, wait for somebody to walk up to the car and ten seconds later they would be on their way back in to the city of Charleston. My people watching skills were on high alert when I spotted a familiar car coming through the manor, I just knew somebody must have gotten in trouble earlier and their parent was about to be notified.

My nosiness got the best of me, even though I was not supposed to leave the porch I had to see where this car was going. Luckily I didn't have to go far, the Jetta went up to the second building of Griffen Drive and stopped, but to my surprise the driver didn't get out. Instead Lil Trey came out. I knew it was Trey because he had the highest high top fade around, and his edge up was always immaculate. Half of the older teenage girls in the manor had a crush on him. He was super funny and always had people laughing whenever he would engage in conversation with them. He had a twin brother that had mysteriously disappeared. Nobody talked about him it was like he just dropped off the face of the earth, his name was Tevin. Tevin was a quiet guy who hardly ever came outside, he stayed in the house and occasionally you would catch him peering out his bedroom window.

Trey walked up on the car with a million-dollar smile. He hopped in the car for about two minutes then got back out. They exchanged words before he headed back in the same building and the car pulled off quickly, the driver went up the hill to turn around in the parking lot. As the car came back down the hill, I stared at the blonde haired lady trying to process what I was for sure had just taken place. Mrs. Hartwell was rummaging through her purse with one hand and clutching her steering wheel with the other as she passed back through the projects.

About ten minutes later Lil Trey came off the hill with Dave, as they passed by pushing each other off the sidewalk, he told him "I'm going to get a room for the night I'll be back tomorrow, white girl came through you know she cop a lot."

"I'm about to start calling you Telly Trey."

They both laughed and walked right on by out of the manor.

"Too Much Of Anything Makes You Addict."
"Sometimes I Rhyme Slow"

PETE ROCK AND C.L SMOOTH

CHAPTER 8: WE CANT BE STOPPED

I already knew I was about to get in trouble. But I couldn't miss this mission, Brannon had convinced us, that Gold was buried in the woods behind the manor. He said, that it was enough for all of us to get rich and move to Disney World. After that statement we were all down to take that trip through the forest that surrounded our neighborhood. It was eight of us and I knew for sure at least six of us were looking at serious whippings when we returned. The woods were a big no no, but we didn't listen we were on a quest for the Magic Kingdom. There was a place at the top filled with quicksand called The Flattop and you were not a true Woo Kid if you didn't attempt to make it to the Flat Top at least once. I was totally unprepared, for one I had on my brand new pair of Jordan's and two I was hungry. I made it to the playground too late to get a free lunch so I grabbed a juice and planned on going to the store momentarily. When Yanni tapped me on the shoulder I already had a feeling who it was. Yanni was my best friend, but we didn't always get along she was aggressive and always on a whole other tip. People always said we favored, the only difference is where my eyes were hazel, hers were coal black. Same height, same build, but totally different attitudes.

"You going to the Flat Top with us or you going to sit on the porch all day with the old women"

I rolled my eyes, "I'll let you know"

"Just say you not going because you'd rather sit and listen to your grandmother and them old ladies talk about bingo."

"Just say you're not sure what I'm going to do because you don't know as much as you think you do."

She walked off and I rolled my eyes once again glad she was gone.

SNAP.

34

I turned around Yanni was over there by the tree looking up at the sun. I hoped an acorn dropped down and knocked some sense into her. She thought she knew it all, you couldn't tell her nothing. The girl had an answer for everything and most of the time it was irrational and illogical. Most of the other kids ignored her, I figured it was because she never had anything nice to say. She waved for me to come over to where she was at, when I made over there... She said "B 52" and busted out laughing.

"Are you about to head up to the woods with us or are you going to hear about how close the bingo crew almost came to winning big last night?"

"For your information my grandmother did good?"

Pointing down to my new Jordan's I skipped in the direction of the kids heading towards the woods. I didn't have to look back to see she was salty. I knew she was, every time I got back smart with her she would give me the silent treatment. For about twenty minutes she would stay in a funky mood, then she would return back to her feisty self. Halfway into the woods, my heart skipped a beat, I wondered if Jason ever came to the projects in West Virginia because Lord knows nobody would hear us scream up there. But since it was Thursday I convinced myself it was safe because Jason only massacred folks on Fridays, and today was nowhere near the 13th. To sum the trip up in a nutshell it was a disaster. We couldn't find the right path to get to the top, but the worst part was we ended up in a patch of quicksand and if my luck couldn't be worse I destroyed my right Jordan. I knew was grandmother was going to have to grab her inhaler from all the yelling she was about to do. I was really considering just staying in the woods and trying to survive off the berry's that grew there. I already knew I had a mouthful coming in epic proportions. Coming out of the woods my heart had sank down in my stomach and landed in my filthy shoe. Chris popped up beside me, put his arm around my shoulder and said "you scared out your mind right now aren't you?"

I nodded, my voice had left me a long time ago.

Brannon, just laughed, "You are always tearing your shoes up, remember we won in the science fair, and you spilled somebody else's experiment all over your shoes?" Brannon was my homie he was really really smart. He was just a hot head as well with crazy ideas, that I sometimes got suckered into, like today.

"Gimme your shoe"

"You not getting my shoe these just came out"

"Oh you can talk now"

"What you going to do with it"

"Just give me the shoe and I'll knock on your uncles back bedroom window when I'm finished with it."

I figured going in the house with one shoe was better than going in with that dirty one.

I handed over my shoes and made a run for my uncle's bedroom window. As I climbed through I hoped he didn't get me for my shoe, because I would make sure my uncle beat him up when he came home from jail.

I walked through the house and it was eerily quiet, everything was calm and the ceiling fan provided the calm cooling that I had been in search of all day. I must have dozed off because my grandmother woke me up snapping her fingers wildly in front of my face.

"You ought to take better care of your stuff"

I was trying to process the scenario so I wouldn't say anything incriminating.

"Here, go put this shoe up, Chris told me he stepped on your shoe and you made him go wipe it off, you could have done that yourself"

"Why do I have to be like this? Momma said I'm priceless

So I am all worthless, starved and it's just for bein' a nice kid

Sometimes I wish I could afford a pistol then, though

Last stop to hell, I would've ended things a while ago"

NAUGHTY BY NATURE "EVERYTHING'S GONNA BE ALRIGHT"

CHAPTER 9: VISION OF LOVE

The summer was in full force, school was out and the Woo was in full effect. Some of the finest girls and prettiest faces could be seen walking around Orchard Manor. LL Cool J must have slid through these streets a time or two when he was making the lyrics to Around the Way Girl. My aunt Vina was the definition of Dope. My grandparents blessed her with smooth honey colored skin, high cheek bones, full lips, brown almond shaped eyes and a thick full head of hair. Her shape was supermodel status and she was project runway fine. She walked the streets in our neighborhood like she was in Fashion Week in Paris. She was fine and she knew it too, the fact that my uncle Plush was a beast with his hands made her feel like she was untouchable, for that reason her mouth was savage. She would vocally wreak havoc on the local boys if she didn't get her way, nobody wanted to deal with her mouth because if they slipped up and came sideways she would run too Plush and he was running pockets and ruining reps so they would just let her go with her flow. My grandmother couldn't stand her attitude and she would physically try to knock it out of her but nothing phased her she was dead set on doing her. She had so many different friends I couldn't keep up with which ones she was cool with at the moment. They were always falling out, over gossip, guys and anything under the sun. I think she loved me when I was a baby but she hated me when I grew into a child. She was mean to me for no reason, but if anybody ever bothered me I knew she was coming full force, ready to get at whoever, however. I just learned to stay out of her way, but when she wasn't home I would sneak into her room put on her clothes and pretend to be her. At one point in time she had a modeling contract but something top secret happened and she had to come home. Nobody would ever say why she returned just my grandmother would mumble something about her "being on some bullshit."

Me and my friends were outside making up dance routines to Another Bad Creation's "At The Playground" Vina was sitting on the porch actually laughing at us and smiling. The breeze was blowing and

38

we were all having a good time. We stopped to take a break and catch our breath and just enjoy each other's company. Tanya, who lived up the hill starting humming the tune of SWV's Weak and everybody got hype. The girl could literally blow, her voice was undeniably awesome and the crazy thing about it was hardly anybody knew she could sing. She didn't do it very often but when she did the girl hit all kinds of notes and riffs just pure raw talent. I loved to hear her sing, cause my singing voice had to be the only thing I inherited from my daddy. It was deep and squeaky and just down right comedic. But on the flip side I had crazy word play and I spit with the best of them. After she finished singing, Mya started beat boxing and it was on. I grabbed a hair brush that was sitting on the stoop and started rhyming

Me myself and don't I need no copyright

Cause when chicks try to bite they don't copyright

I'm like fat chicks in small jeans I'm that tight

304 Orchard Manor Woo Baby born and raised

You on the bench and I'm calling out the plays

Let me lace up my jays

Call me coach, our apartment clean isn't never seen a roach

Spray you wit my water gun now you super soaked

Cold world throwing on ya starter coat

I'm a diamond you can keep ya gold ropes

If you think you better than me you must be smoking dope.......

I saw stars and landed in the grass. I couldn't do nothing but get up and laugh my grandmother had come up behind me and hit me for saying smoking dope. Everybody was laughing and cheering because she had started dancing and next thing you know she had us all lined up at the ice cream truck. She bought everybody red white and blues and now we were back on the stoop in high spirits. Everybody except my aunt, she had a gaze that could turn anything in to stone at that moment. My eyes scanned the entire front block and I couldn't find what had her on tip. I saw a few young dudes mugging a black BMW and whispering amongst themselves under the tree by Smallridge Court. I know they weren't even on Vina's radar so I couldn't figure it out. It took a minute to see what she was staring at, the dude from out of town she supposedly was talking to, was in the BMW with someone else. Mad I wasted four minutes of my life and my professional people watching skills on this wack mess, I rolled my eyes, he was ugly anyways.

"He ugly Vina."

She actually laughed, cracking a smile at me, "You damn right he is!"

"I don't care about the other girls, just be good to me!

But if I ever saw one, that would be the end

He couldn't kick the storyline that she was just a friend

The girls I didn't care, fine legs don't lie

See cause Georgie was into making your girls cry"

"Georgie Porgie" MC Lyte

CHAPTER 10: IM READY

I was trying to my hardest to convince my grandmother to allow me to go to my friend Tate's party at his house tonight. Even though I wasn't technically invited our parents were good friends so I knew it wouldn't be a problem. Anne was not having it.

"Those parties are for the older kids, so you might as well hang it up missy."

"Not tonight it's going to be people my age there. I'm going to be the only person not there."

"Invite one of your friends over."

"They're all going."

"I bought you a new book start reading that."

"I don't want to read it tonight I want to go to the party, whyyyyyyyyy are you being so mean."

"Ask me again and you're going to find out what mean is. I said No! and that's what I mean it's too much going on up the hill after dark and it's no place for kid to be. Maybe next year."

My brain stopped, did she say *next year*, clearly she lost her mind. I had to wait until next summer to go to dance party, this was pure madness. I stomped to the back room, my Granddaddy was cracking up and hitting his knee. He looked at me with tears in his eyes.
"I am not getting in to this one. Did you hear how her voice changed when she said MAYBE NEXT YEAR. Leave that woman alone."
I folded my arms. And left out the room

He yelled out, "go get some cards I'll play you in crazy 8's."

I smiled, I loved playing cards with my grandfather even though I knew he cheated. He even switched cards when he was playing me and I

wasn't even that good. We played cards for a while, he won every game and was talking major junk the whole time. It got hot in the apartment and I went on the porch to catch the nighttime breeze. I was sitting there with my eyes closed when I felt a presence in front of me. I opened my eyes to see Yanni standing there looking overwhelmed,
"Where have you been all day."

"In the house resting for this party tonight."

I must have had a crazy look on my face because she smirked "why the sour face"

I was trying to figure out how she got an invite and I didn't. I for sure was not about to tell her that I wasn't allowed to go. But I'm sure she already peeped game by the way she was smiling deviously.

"You on porch punishment again"
"Nope I'm just sitting out here before I go start my new book."

"I forgot you were a nerd."

"Memory is everything, if you can't remember the simple stuff how can you handle anything major."

She shook her head, "you're really like the reincarnation of a sixty-year-old woman."

I got up and started doing The Butterfly and we both laughed.

"Let's go for a walk."

I thought about it, my grandmother was at Bingo and my Granddaddy was knocked out in his room. They didn't say I couldn't leave the porch just that I couldn't go to the party. So I decided as long as I made it back down the hill before my grandmother came home I was good as gold. We took the long way around the manor, and I should have known Yanni was on some mess because we ended up right in front of Tate's building. The music was blasting, and we ran over to the window to look in, but we couldn't see anything because the lights were off. All you could see was silhouettes grinding up against each other, to the sound of Color Me Bad. My eyes were glued to the screen I hadn't seen nothing like this before, this was getting very interesting.

I turned around to see if Yanni was ready to dip and to my surprise she was nowhere to be found. I figured she had slid in the party without me since she was invited. I was beyond heated, that girl was an idiot. How was she going to leave me up in the Circle at night by myself? That's what I get for coming up here. I took a deep breath and walked in the party.

As soon as I walked in the first person I seen was Chris all over Kristee on the wall. He looked at me, then I guess he had to do a double take to make sure it was me. I don't know why but I was instantly pissed when I saw him with her, she had a darn sock on her head that was holding on for dear life. He walked over to me with a crooked smile on his face. Now it was my turn to do a double take he had hopped fresh on me since the last time I seen him. He had on some blue jean shorts with black leather on the front, black high top Fila's, and a gold rope setting off his black tee. His fade was crispy and his skin was super clear. I couldn't help but smile.

"Boy you looking like you all that and a bag of chips"

He laughed. "Era you are such a cornball you don't even sound right trying to spit game."

My face instantly turned up. I threw my hand up.

"See I was just saying you looked straight, but you can talk to the hand with me ever trying to spit game at you."

He shrugged his shoulders "I'm just trying to get like you, fly every day"

I laughed, "you know my grandmother keep a layaway in all year round."

We both cracked up. But soon as I said her name I felt like Cinderella of the hood. I had to get back and Yanni was nowhere in sight.

"Walk me down the hill it's dark and my friend left me."

"Who you come with?"

"Yanni!"

"Who?"

I didn't have time for his games. Acting like he didn't know who she was when I was trying to make it back to the porch before my grandmother got home. I just blinked at him real hard and he headed to the door. I followed behind him as he dapped a few people up along the way. Before he made it to the door, Sock Head was all in his face trying to grind again. He whispered something in her and she backed off with a smile. That smile instantly changed into a smug look when she saw me behind him, as I passed by her and her friends she muttered, "oh look who slid off the porch."

The music stopped on cue and everybody heard her. I did not have time for this my grandmother was probably heading home now. She must have needed the attention because she said it again.

"Oh you slid off the porch boo."

See.
I just couldn't ever go somewhere without some extra stuff. I was not about to do this with her. I looked her up and down before I smiled and told her, "you just worry about that sock not sliding off that baby pony tail, while you in here grinding so hard."

Everybody fell out laughing before Chris pulled me out the door.

I looked back to see her with the dummy face.

"Hahahahahhahaahhahaha! Chris laughed half way down the

hill. "Why you roll up like that and interrupt my set then try to go on baby girl like that?"

"You know she started it."
     "But you went stupid hard for no reason yo."

     "They get on my nerves, they always coming for me because my people strict. I'm done letting stuff slide."

     Soon as I said the word slide again, we both fell out laughing all the way to my grandparent's porch. We sat on the porch cracking jokes on each other until my grandmother hopped out of her friends Honda with her bingo bag. She scrunched her face up when she saw me.

     "What are you doing out here this late?"

     "Nothing, talking to Chris"

     She smiled once she saw him, then she started instantly plunking him upside his head. He was ducking her, laughing and covering his face. Next thing you know she started hitting him with her bingo bag and he was still laughing. I was trying to figure out what in the tarnation did she get so worked up for.

     "Mrs. Anne why you buggin?"
She put her hands on hips. Looked him up and down, and it was clear she had peeped his new gear as well.

     "Boy I'm not dumb I've seen it all, and I know you can't afford all that with your 7th grade budget. Now be silly if you want to and end up where Luke and all the rest of them are. Now get off my porch in ten minutes or I'm coming back out to beat you some more."
     She popped him once more before she went in the house.

Chris just shook his head, "she crazy but I know what I'm doing. I'm stacking all summer and then I'm done. I'm going to play ball when school starts and keep my grades up so I can get into a good college. This just a summer job."

The way he said it made sense to me. It wasn't like he was trying to be the next neighborhood superstar he was just trying to not worry about where his next meal was coming from and keep his little brothers straight.

He stood up and smoothed his shirt out, rubbing an imaginary goatee he looked at me and said, "imma make it to league watch"

I just smiled.

A car pulled up and stopped right in front of the building. Chris threw two fingers up and the window came down, to reveal Zeke's face. Zeke was a super dark chocolate dude with a low cut Caesar with deep jet black waves. Zeke yelled out the window "I see you got your hands full man."

I rolled my eyes not sure what he meant by that.

"Nah it isn't that type of party," he said with hint of aggression I couldn't place.

Zeke nodded, "I already know you see her eyes, if she isn't already she gonna grow up and be a stone cold heartbreaker."

I wished he would let off his breaks and pull off he was stone cold annoying already and hadn't been in my presence a good two minutes. Sensing my irritation, Chris told him he would get up with him later tonight.

"Make sure you handle that situation before morning."

Chris nodded. And I saw something flicker in his eyes and then fade.

Zeke skirted off leaving a cloud of smoke which brought my grandmother back on the porch, she told me to tell Chris goodnight and come in.

"Bye scaredy cat"

"Thanks for walking me back and I know you wasn't trying to scuff up your new Fila's"

He looked me in my face and said, "I do my dirty work in my Hi Tec boots!" then he hit me with

"I know you not scared I heard you was out here socking niggas"

"The only sock you should be worried about is your lil girlfriends."

He hollered out in laughter and took off running back in to the darkness up the hill.

Do you know, where ya goin to

Do like the things that life is showin you

"A Teenage Love" Slick Rick

CHAPTER 11: CREEPIN ON AH COME UP

For some odd reason I couldn't sleep, I could not get comfortable in my uncles bed. I had taken over his room ever since he went to jail, it was full of pictures, rap posters and it was just my style. I heard some arguing at the front of the building and got up to see what was going on.

The black BMW from earlier was parked in the same spot it was when Vina copped her attitude. It was a heated argument coming from the car, a female voice was yelling about getting played and the guy was telling her to calm down. I saw two figures come from around the building and run up on both sides of the car. I closed the blinds, knowing nothing good was about to happen and I was not about to have nightmares.

My aunt lived near a cemetery, and from time to time my friends and I would stay up there. At night we would tell ghost stories, then get to scared to fall asleep. When I returned to the manor I would have nightmares for days. So I could only imagine what seeing some real life wild stuff would do to me.

I went back to my uncle's room, and a few minutes later there was a loud banging on the door. It was HySeem the guy from the BMW, he was leaking blood from his head and asking my grandmother for some towels. He didn't want her to call the paramedics he just needed to get cleaned up because he had just been robbed. He said he didn't know who did it all he knew was he had gotten stomped out by somebody in some Hi-Tec boots and a face mask. I stopped dead in my tracks after that last sentence and shook my head.

My grandmother helped him clean his wounds, but my grandfather never came out of the bedroom to see what all the commotion was about, which was odd to me. He usually was the first one to jump to action, but maybe he thought he was ugly too.

He thanked my grandmother and told her he would look out for her later on because whoever got him, jacked him for 5 bands, his jewelry, phone and he didn't have any money on him to give to her.

When he left I went in the living room, my grandmother looked exhausted, she told me to go pour her some Pepsi and turn off the light. I did as she asked and headed back to my uncle's room. I stopped in front of Vina's room pushed the door open and she was knocked out with a 40 oz. in her windowsill. Even though she got on my nerves I'm glad she wasn't in that car anything could have happened. I wanted to wake her up to tell her the ugly boy had a knot on his head and not in his pocket. But I knew how ugly waking her up out her sleep for anything could get. I went back to my uncle's room and the curtains were blowing like crazy. I didn't remember opening the window that far, but the breeze was calming and it felt heavenly. I walked over closer to the bed and saw a pair of black Fila's in the window sill.

You can't be any geek off the street

gotta be handy with the steel if you know what I mean, earn your keep!

REGULATORS!!! MOUNT UP!

NATE DOGG & WARREN G

CHAPTER 12: REASONABLE DOUBT

School started back, I was in the seventh grade, and low key terrified. The school was ten minutes away from the manor. Man this was like a whole new world for me, I was ready to explore, but it was just crazy because I had an iron clad routine in the manor but change was good sometimes. I knew what was up, this was all new to me. But one thing I learned quick, whether we liked each other in the Woo or not, at school we were a clique. Ten million strong and growing. I knew a few kids that weren't from the manor and I soon began to develop other friendships but the bond that grew between those intertwined in those bricks was a separate entity in itself.

I suffered from severe culture shock, at Stonewall Jackson Middle School. Some of the kids there had the lives you saw on television shows. I was intrigued with people who lived Lifetime movie lives. I didn't know who to feel sorry for them or me. Them for having to live so boring and not being appreciative of the grind or the struggle. Or me for not having the sense to realize nobody wants to struggle. The struggle is designed to make us think that it's normal, so we will be complacent and not exceed the level of comfortability to become a representative of our own true selves. Stuck in a system that keeps certain individuals stagnant in growth.

I experienced the weirdness first hand, the black kids who lived in regular houses and apartments sometimes acted as if they were superior to us. It blew my mind because I wasn't trying to compare differences until they made it noticeable. And it was usually the ones who couldn't hold a candle to us. Their furniture was worn, clothes recycled, and grades subpar but thought just because we lived in public housing they would place us at the lowest of the totem pole. Clearly they had us confused because stars were bred over that way every day. I had gained a now found respect for my neighbors we were truly persevering amidst our adversities. Middle school was actually a challenge and I didn't get bored as easily as I did in elementary, which a major plus for me.

Chris kept his word, he joined the football team towards the end of the summer. I saw him hanging out in the neighborhood less often and spending more time in the gym. I never asked him about that night and to this day his shoes are still in the back of the closet.

One day after school, we were sitting on a bench on Bowman Court, it was quite a few people outside just kicking it. Tanika and Londa were filling me in about the drama I had been missing lately on their side of the neighborhood. There was a pretty girl named Shayla who was about sixteen years old, she had two older brothers Marcus and Daniel who did not play about nothing that had to do with her. Shayla came from a whole family of sharks, you felt the bite before you ever saw them coming. Shayla was light skin, long brown hair, dark brown eyes and curves that belonged on a 24-year-old woman. Shayla's brothers kept her decked out in the latest, her hair was always done but she never she really had any close friends outside of her family. She was ten times more sheltered than me. Whenever she came outside it was never alone, and it wasn't ever for long period of time. She went to some private school downtown, so she rarely had any interaction with us at all. Sometimes she would sit outside when we made up dance routines, laughing and clapping. Their mother Ms. Bernadette worked two jobs so she was never home, leaving Shayla in the care of her older brothers. They lived on the first floor of building 320. Each building had 3 floors with two apartments on each floor, the stairwell going up the middle seen a lot of action, and apparently I had been missing it all.

The game that had been going on at the basketball court by the creek must have ended because now Bowman was packed with all the fellas. Ace and Ronnie made their way over to the bench to sit with us. BJ started to come over, but once he saw me he went the other way. We cracked jokes about old times and made fun of each other. I was looking for my lip gloss when I felt eyes on me. I looked up to see Juan staring, he was at least twenty-three and a creeper for sure. I don't know what it was about him, but whenever he looked at me I always felt extremely uncomfortable. I stayed clear of him for that reason alone, something about him rubbed me the wrong way. He was always just looking, with a half grin on his face, either he was slow or he was thinking about something he had no business. I was willing to bet my allowance it was the latter. Juan got money, I don't know how but he was always decked out in the latest, he was the flyest loner in the hood. Whatever he was doing it must have been dolo because he never ran with a crew or with the fellas, he was around but never in the mix. All he ever did was watch what everybody else was doing.

Imagine our surprise when Shayla walked out of her building, dressed in white daisy dukes, a white tank top and sparkling white shell toe Adidas and headed in our direction. We all had the same look on our face, like who let the Sugar Lady out, because her family acted as if she would melt if she stayed outside to long. Well we were about to find out why they had her under such a tight leash.

Shayla came over to our bench sat on the outer circle and said Hi, then looked up at the sky and closed her eyes. Tanika whispered in my ear "Poor child doesn't get outside often she doesn't know what the sun feels like."

Ronnie was staring at her thick thighs cascading out the sides of her shorts, he was close to drooling on her leg, the way his bottom lip was hanging. Ace called him out on it.

"Damn homie, breathe before you go into cardiac arrest out"

Everybody laughed but Shayla and Ronnie.

Ronnie immediately cut into Ace "long as you don't breathe that hot shit you been blowing in people's face all day."

"You're always getting in your feelings knowing you can't handle the heat so don't start nothing you not trying to finish. Especially when you got on my shirt, matter of fact takes it off, that might help you cool off."

"Take it off of me" Ronnie said rising up.

"Nah, give it to me folded up like it was when you got it out my drawer."

I couldn't believe they were about to take it there.

Tonika spoke up before I did "y'all need to quit it trying to show off for somebody that's not paying neither one of y'all any attention."

I looked over at Shayla and to my amazement she was smiling at Juan, he was licking his lips like a bootleg LL Cool J.

Me and Londa exchanged confused looks, and Tonika who was becoming a serial whisperer, was back in my ear "that's why she came over here, she thinks she slick."

It was obvious that they had something weird going on, but something wasn't right with Shayla all she did was smile at the sky and then at Juan.

I was happy he stopped staring at me and he had his full attention on the Shayla the star gazer.

Tonika asked her "what school do you go to girl?"

She smiled and said "I go to a big private school, my daddy sends me and pays for it. He said the schools everybody else goes to don't care about kids like me."

There was complete silence around the bench nobody said nothing. Shayla was special needs. At that moment we all immediately looked at Juan, like if you don't get on her weirdo.

I became instantly concerned, "are you home by yourself Shayla?"

She just smiled.

Oh gosh? I guess I was playing babysitter until her brothers got back because she clearly shouldn't be left in the house or outside by herself. She was halfway in a daze and it was intriguing to me, she was beautiful and innocent even in a place, like this where most of us had become slightly jaded.

She came over and sat, beside me still smiling. Picking up my notebook she grabbed my pencil, and started flipping through my poems until she found an empty page. She began drawing a really good picture of a butterfly. I was impressed the girl had skills.

"You did that, sign the bottom of it for me." She scribbled her name at the bottom.

The sound of the ice cream truck had everyone on their feet. It was much needed; the sun had been serving major rays on the court all day in epic proportions. I looked at Shayla who was still smiling and perfecting her drawing, "you want an ice cream cone?"

She clapped her hands and smiled even bigger. Which actually made me smile.

I told her to stay right there, I headed across the street to get her a cone. I looked back and she was looking happier than I had ever seen her looking staring from her bedroom window. I didn't turn around in time and bumped into Londa spilling all my change in the street. I picked it up and noticed Juan being a creep as usual, watching me bend over to pick up my change. I shuddered in disgust. Londa noticed it too and said "he needs help."

I wanted to give him the middle finger but somebody might see me and go tell my grandparents.

I prepared my mind for some of this delicious ice cream. I wanted a banana split but I wouldn't have enough for me and Shayla to get some so, I settle for two cones instead.

While in line Tanika and Londa began discussing the fact that she must be miserable. She's always in the house even though she's "special" she shouldn't be bored all the time. We decided we would invite her outside to sit with us more often. Hell I felt like I was about to start my own Babysitters Club.

After getting the ice cream we walked back across the street only to find out Shayla had left and I was distraught she left my precious notebook on the bench. See that's why I didn't for people to touch my book because they didn't appreciate the greatness that was enclosed in those pages.

Where did that girl go?

I wanted to make sure she got her ice cream so I walked over to her building and knocked on the door. I heard movement inside the apartment so I knocked a little harder. Right before I was about to give up, a boy about eleven came to the door rubbing the sleepiness from eyes.

"Can you give this to Shayla?" I handed him the ice cream.

"She left with my cousins they should be back in a few" he said licking the cone that was not for him. I wanted to smack it out of his hand. *Little BeBe Kid.*

I turned to walk off, but something wouldn't let me. I had a few questions. "How long they been gone?"

"About 45 minutes"

"Nah you need you to call them, Shayla was outside with us after they pulled off and now she's nowhere to be found."

My last statement had the young boy alarmed and on edge, he ran to the house phone dialed a number and clutched his forehead. "I thought shay shay left with y'all she not in here and she not outside"

There was yelling on the other end of the phone. He hung up and went into panic mode. The boy ran past me outside, up and down the court in every building, but nobody remembered seeing her get up.

We had covered the whole court yelling her name, with no luck we headed to the back side of the buildings.

Still no Shayla.

"Shaylaaaaaaaaaa"

My heart began to beat faster hoping that she didn't make it out to the Main Street. But I'm sure somebody would have seen her leaving the manor if that was the case. By the time we made it back around to our initial spot, her brothers Marcus and Daniel were wreaking pure havoc on the doors on Bowman Court.

They knocked on every door in every building but nobody saw her.

Daniel who could have passed for Shayla's twin had a vein protruding from his forehead that gave a clear indication that his brain was on overload. He was darn near talking to himself.

He paused for a minute then went over to the little boy who answered the door, spoke with him briefly then headed over to us.

"Who was Shay Shay outside with?"

"She came out on her own, but she sat here with us the whole time. I asked her if she wanted some ice cream, she smiled and clapped, so I told her stay right here until I came back When I left she was drawing in my notebook. I came back the notebook was there but she wasn't."

"How long were you at the truck?"

"About three minutes the line wasn't that long."

He rubbed his head, "she couldn't have gotten that far in three minutes."

Marcus kicked a rocked that was on the ground in front of him. He looked like he was ready to set it off at any given moment.

"Who was out here that isn't out here now?" Daniel looked at me, Tanika, Londa, Ace and Ronnie like we were his last resort, basically pleading for us to try and recollect any type of useful information that could help.

We scanned the court trying to see if anybody else had dipped off, it looked like the same group of people. We couldn't come up with anything, and Daniel looked extra stress.

Mr. Ray came over asking for change. He was always drunk and always begging, the rumor was he used to be in the NFL but he started shooting up and was cut from the team. He was overly aggressive with his bumming, he acted like you had to give him your extra change, which was part of the reason he was always getting cursed out. I stood up to move closer, to Tonika and get away from the pungent smell of liquor seeping through his pores. The way he looked me up and down gave me a feeling of déjà vu. Before I could put my finger on it, Londa grabbed Marcus's arm "Juan was out here when we left and he was looking at your sister just like Ray just did."

Ray took major offense to her statement.

"Shut your mouth and learn some respect, making the wrong assumptions could put content on given day!" he gazed into her eyes, but she wasn't hearing it.

She sucked her teeth, "y'all old men disgusting and weird."

Daniel pushed past Ray before their exchange could continue any further. He went up to building 208 and starting kicking on a door so crazy a small crowd had gathered around.

He banged on the door until finally Marcus tapped on the door with his fist, and said "you got five seconds to open this door or I'mma empty every clip I own through every window in this bitch."

The door swung open on the count of two.

Juan stepped out and they ran through the apartment but came out without Shayla.

"You see my sister nigga"

"She was on the court when I left"

"Did you leave before or after Mrs. Anne's granddaughter went to the ice cream truck."

"Way before then"

"When did you leave?"

"Don't exactly remember but the truck hadn't come yet when I left." Marcus was asking all of the questions but Juan was only looking at Daniel whenever he answered them.

"He is lying!" Londa yelled from outside the building. "He was staring Era down when she dropped her changed by the truck. He was still out there when the truck was out there. I remember."

Marcus yanked Juan out the apartment into the stairwell. Daniel went back in the apartment and came out empty handed again.

Daniel got up so close to Juan's face I'm sure he could read his mind. Juan looked at Daniel, and for a brief moment there was awkward silence between the two. Daniel put his face close to Juan's head and said "I wish you would." Whatever Juan was about to say he quickly changed his mind.

Juan opened his mouth again but Marcus cut him off.

"These kids don't have a reason to lie, but you do. And I find it suspect as a mother fucker that your always outside watching these young girls play but never on the court or the field with real niggas."

He rubbed his chin, "Now I'm going to find my sister and if I find out you had anything to do with her pulling this little disappearing act. I'm going to break your mother fucking jaw, and black both your eyes. So the next time you think about looking at a young girl you have flash backs of the ass whipping I'm about to put on you." Marcus reached over Daniel and told him, "I'm not using my hands for shit but to let one go right in your dick, now let my sister not surface in next ten minutes."

As if on cue Shayla came from around the back side of the building smiling as big and bright as ever.

Marcus ran over to her, checking to make sure she was alright, he quizzed her, "Butterfly where you been?"
She smiled.

"Butterfly where did you go?"

She smiled, "I colored a picture like at school." She pulled an envelope out of her pocket. Marcus smiled when he saw a bunch of butterflies drawn to perfection on the paper. When he flipped it over his face turned stoic, then the vein returned to his forehead. He tossed the envelope over to Daniel. Daniel's face was just blank, like he passed out in his body. Marcus snatched the envelope from Daniel and smacked Juan in the face with it then proceeded to stomped him out. Daniel and Marcus beat the hell out of Juan in the hallway and nobody intervened, Shayla smiled the whole time. She walked over towards the front entrance and picked up the envelope, she brought it back to where we stood. I noticed the address on it belonged to Juan's mother.

She must have gone out the back door, while he pretended to not have seen her at all.

She was totally clueless to the situation, I wondered what happened to her during the time we were looking for her.

Her brothers came out of the hallway breathing heavily, Marcus still managed to be gentle with her.

"Butterfly lets go home"

She looked at me, "Ice Cream?"

I smiled and said "next time you can walk with me."

Marcus nodded his head at me, "y'all girls stay away from dude he isn't right, if he ever come at any of y'all sideways again come holla at me."

Later on that night somebody filled up that same very apartment with bullets. Juan stopped coming outside afterwards.

"I don't even know you and I'd kill you myself

You played with her like a doll and put her back on the shelf"

Love Is Blind- EVE

CHAPTER 13: ALL EYEZ ON ME

School was actually going good, I had to give a speech in my creative writing class on the American Dream. I walked up to the front of the class, and I knew that my version of the assignment was probably not what Mrs. Caldwell had in mind when she did her lesson plan. Needless to say I jumped right in to it....

I took a deep breath.

"Woo Baby I was born and bred in the gutter

Never was infatuated with Butta's

My mind was to grown to live fast to get robbed at Young's

They told me to shut up when the power was in my tongue

And Ronnie told me hit the windmill but don't ever run

They were chasing boys and my mental was on some other

Make it big so I can take care of my mother

I almost believed em when they said in trying wasnt no use

But Mr. John said these buildings and these bricks aint no excuse

So I refused what they were telling us

Once I realized the system was failing us

My homies should have had degrees,

A few should have been in the league

But they were intrigued by the streets

I won't knock the hustle That's how the cards shuffled

But they all know regardless that I love em

Never been perfect but never been in too much trouble

Ima speak up and for them I wont mumble

I see the struggle and decided I want double

Some for me and some for she

That gave up or just never made it

For the ones who's dreams faded

They say never forget where you came from

Well this is where I got the game from

And it's nothing that I'm ashamed of

Wouldn't pretend that I believe in the American dream

The picket fences or the matching color schemes

My reality is built off childhood memories

Of big money dreams not government cheese

Or rehabilitation for the mind not just the fiends

Laundromats for the heart and the streets are clean

They tell me leave that behind me

How when my dreams remind me

That I could me a statistic but somehow I barely missed it

I guess I'm an abnormality of logistics

But to be specific

The lights don't impress me and what you are suggesting

is to forget what made me

Well your suggestions don't phase me

They know what it is I bleed and breathe the Woo

I just needed time to do what I have to do

But don't ever think I'm not coming back for you

Because for any and every kid with a dream I am proof.........   "

Mrs. Cardwell clapped and she told me "You Rock Girl"

      I almost broke out into the Typewriter but I was a part of the Rhythmless Nation. I couldn't catch a beat if it landed on me. The announcements came over the intercom and the results for Homecoming Court were in. I literally passed out in my seat when my name was called. I couldn't believe it, I couldn't wait to get home and tell my grandmother. I don't remember anything that happened in school after that. I just couldn't wait to walk across that field.

      I doubt the bus had fully parked but I hopped off it, and ran all the way to my grandmother's porch. Her and a few of her bingo buddies were sitting outside.

      "Guess What!"

      "What little girl?"

      "I made 7th grade Homecoming Court, I get to walk the field during the Homecoming Game!" She jumped up gave me a big hug and told me to go get the cordless phone. She called everybody in our family from Cleveland, Detroit, to Washington, D.C.

"We have to go find you something to wear this weekend, and get you some dress shoes!" I sat on the porch feeling like Whitney Houston, I should have known something foul was about to happen. My day was going too good.

I walked up the hill to my mother's apartment I couldn't wait to tell her. I was almost there when I saw Kristee and her crew. She was still salty about all the disses I threw her way about that sock during Tate's party this summer. She was dusty and I was determined to not let her get on my nerves today.

"Congratulations on Homecoming," she said, surprising me.

"Thank you!" I answered with a sincere smile.

"I'm sure all the nerds decided to stick together and elect one of their own"

Oh, this was what she was on today. Alright my mood changed instantly. "Whoever voted for me, I'm appreciative of them. And it might not have been all nerds because last time I checked there was nothing cute about being a dummy."

"I hope you don't think Chris is walking you across that field big head."

"So that's why you're in feelings, worried about somebody walking me across a field when you might not ever make it to walk across a stage and get a diploma little head."

"I'd rather have a little head than that big rock you have sitting on your neck straining your shoulders."

Her crew fell out laughing.

"You almost need a helmet, aren't you in the seventh grade for the second time? You had two chances to make Homecoming and failed at both. Maybe next year, you know they say third times the charm. Pretty soon you'll be able to do 7th grade orientation all by yourself!"

"You sure act like you know me like you watching my life."

"Actually I don't care about your life you came at me. I'm over it I'm about to go home and watch 7th Heaven."

A few of her friends chuckled.

She turned around to walk off then turned back around and punched me dead in my eye.

BAMM!

I think my socket touched the back of my head for six seconds. Once I regained my vision. She was nowhere to be found. Her or her wannabees. I was beyond pissed. I wanted to yell out curse words, but too many of my grandfather's friends lived up this way.

I stomped all the way home, nursing my eye with the palm of my hand. I ended up getting in trouble for getting socked in the eye. Explain to me how that works, my mom's theory was I should have avoided her all together or hit her first. I told her I never saw it coming, which of course didn't matter. She was just fussing about if I was going to have a black eye or not walking across the field. When I came out the kitchen with a homemade ice pack she was on the phone with Vina, who of course was threatening to go put that work in on Kristee's mama. I could hear her screaming through the phone, about how this was going to stop today. My mom totally flipped the script on her and started talking about Victor Newman. All my mom really did was go to work, clean up the house and play the best jams. Her music collection was the illest around, that's how I ended up knowing all the lyrics to the throwback and ole school jams. I used to love when she used to clean up and Karen White's "Superwoman" would come blaring through the speakers. I would run to the mirror and get my sing on "Early in the morning I put breakfast on youuuuuuuuuuuuuuuur table."

I had to give it to her she had our apartment looking real nice. Her interior decorating skills were on point. I'm sure she thought she was a Chancellor living in Genoa City, she was a certified Young & The Restless addict, Danielle Walters would not miss an episode come hell or high water. I guess that's not too bad considering what some of the other kid's parents were addicted to. I was finally understanding what my grandfather was trying to tell me about the Pipe Dream and crack. He would often say that the white rock was fading the natural love we had for one another. Even though our community was struggling and impoverished we still lived a village lifestyle, folks would look out for one another and the elders would chastise any neighborhood kid caught doing wrong. But once crack hit, the younger generation became disrespectful and doggish to anybody in authority and especially women. The Woo was embarked in its own civil war, times were changing and it was all about the money, power and respect. There was no time to be shook, like Mobb Deep's infamous hook "cause ain't no such things as halfway crooks"

The Woo had turned into a Gold Mine, as the demand for crack grew so did the drama that came along with it. Parents were neglecting their children to chase the almighty high, and children were chasing stability in the almighty dollar. It was a vicious cycle, one that would destroy the already broken down dynamics of the black home. The smoke from the crack pipe was creating a haze of confusion that would leave many casualties when the smoke cleared. I got my notebook out and started writing.

I don't believe you when you say it's just entertainment

When its sunny outside and the weatherman says it raining

When you send money to mars and build invisible cars

when the elderly pays for medicine and damn near starve

When 90 percent of the ...boys I grew up is behind bars

When Keisha had a baby at fourteen by a 30-year-old who was never charged

When Michael went to the middle east and came back emotionally scarred

When nobody can be soft hearted because times is hard

And the news tells you only what they want you to know

Sure your mind wont question what your mind doesn't know

Your eyes can't see when your brain is blind

Kids are just hyper but they say need Ritalin

Soon as your kids stare fidgeting that handed em a prescription to fix em

Now little Carl is cool and calm and he is always chilling

The pharmaceutical companies are making a killing

And we really are a project trapped with them buildings

On American soil or was it over Saudi Arabian oil

With Civil Wars going to war

Or the steroids pumped in the chicken that makes your insides spoil

The contaminated water that they don't tell you to boil

Cause the chemicals cause cancer

But you ignore all that because you want to be a video dancer

You see the flashing lights and dream under the street lights

That someday you'll be famous and rich

Before you know it you'll be 40 still broke and poor

Screaming aint life a b****

CHAPTER 14: JUICE

I was so happy it was Saturday and I could sleep in, I was laying in my bed watching one of my favorite shows *Saved by The Bell!* Luckily my eye didn't turn black or swell, my hazel eyes were a little bit on the green side this morning. I wondered if that was a sign that I could get some money out of my mom. I wanted to go to Rite Aid so I could get the new Word Up! Magazine with Bone Thugs N Harmony on the cover, I was hoping and praying they had a large pullout poster in the middle. It wasn't like my walls weren't already covered with the faces of Krayzie, Layzie, Bizzy, Wish and Flesh. While most girls my age where having crushes on Usher Raymond and R&B singers, I was totally engulfed in rap music. I had a notebook filled with nothing but Bone Lyrics, I studied their lyrics, I memorized their biographies and I was determined that they were going to be famous. Suddenly the thought of sleeping in wasn't so appealing I had to get that magazine before it sold out. *"Moooooooooooooooooom"*

"What the hell is your problem," she huffed busting through my door with a hand full of towels.

"I need that new magazine with Bone on the cover."

"You gonna be broken bone if you ever yell at me like that again for a damn magazine."

"Can I please have six dollars"

"No"

"Are you just saying no because you can"

She looked at me, and blinked.

"This is really important to me."

I wasn't about to let her just say no without a valid reason.

"NO, you running around here getting punched in the eye and you think I'm about to be rewarding you?"

"I didn't start it, you are acting like I punched her? Why am I in trouble again?"

She always said no, I wasn't the least bit surprised, I got up, showered, dressed and headed towards my grandparents. Even if they said no I was sure, I could scuffle up six dollars in change with no problem from the living room couch alone.

When I arrived at my grandmother's doorstep I was shocked to find the door locked and everybody gone, this was rare somebody was usually always there. My blood pressure shot up, I was for sure hoping the magazine wouldn't be gone before they returned. I started pacing back and forth on the walk way in front of the apartment in deep thought about how I was going to get this magazine. The sun was doing the most on my freshly shined Vaseline skin courtesy of my mama. I couldn't take it anymore I was starting to get dizzy and dehydrated, I had actually managed to work myself up over a Centerfold. I walked down to the tree and sat on the steps underneath it. The breeze and shade immediately calmed my nerves. That feeling of peace didn't last long. I heard voices on the other side of the tree. I peek around it to see Kristee and her crew laughing and slowly approaching. She was the reason I wasn't getting my magazine and she for sure was about to pay for it.

When she reached the tree I jumped down and connected my right fist with her jaw. It took her a few seconds to realize what happened before she lunged at me trying to grab my braids. I took my foot and kicked her off the sidewalk and into the street. She stumbled over the curb, and landed on all fours, I wasn't even about to do anything else, when her friend Natalie caught me with a nice right hook in my lip. I grabbed Nisha by the neck, but Kristee managed to get up and catch me with several blows in the back of the head.

PSSSHHHHHHEEEEEZZZZZHHHHHHHHHHHH

Mrs. Ernestine was hanging out of window blowing her whistle hard as hell.
We all stopped instantly to look up at her.

She yelled at us. "Stop that Bullshit and act like young ladies instead of savages. Get some respect about yourselves out here fighting in the street. If you want to fight for something fight for a chance to get out of this deteriorating hell hole."

She blew her whistle once more then slammed her window closed so hard I'm surprised it didn't shatter.

Kristee and I stood there staring at each other, she didn't really want to fight anymore I saw it in all in her face. I didn't want to fight in the first place but I had to let her know I wasn't scared of none of them.
"Leave me alone and I'll leave you alone."

"You got it." she looked me up and down as if she was trying to talk herself out of saying more, then she just nodded her head and began to walk off.

I don't know where Yanni came from, I hadn't seen her in months, but she popped up beside me.

"Yo Nisha got your lip on swole, I seen y'all going at it from up hill."

I felt my lip with my tongue. It felt slightly swollen.

I ran up behind them and pushed Nisha into Kristee, Kristee fell down and Nisha landed on top of her. I mushed Nisha's whole face into Kristee's back.

"Stay out stuff that don't concern you."

She reached up and slapped me into the middle of next week. They both went to work on me. I was trying to regain my composure when Yanni came to my rescue.

"GET UP OFF OF HER NOW, ONE ON ONE"

It wasn't Yanni it was Vina.

Oh gosh.

"Who going first, y'all not about to jump this one!"

PSDDZZZZZZZZZZZZZZZHEWWWWWWWWWW

Everybody stopped dead in their tracks, Mrs. Ernestine was back in her window with the whistle.

Once Vina realized she blew a whistle she fell out laughing, I knew she was crazy. She looked right up at the window and laughed harder. She waved her hand and yanked me all the way to the porch.

"Dummy why was you going to try and fight all the girls by yourself?"

"I had to get her back for yesterday"

"Why didn't you wait until your friends came around so you could at least make sure it was fair! Isn't nothing more dangerous than a jealous chick and trust me it's plenty of those around here, because they on the outside looking in. You can make the worst look good and that's all they see, so of course they gonna hate. And please believe hate will get you hurt. Don't be scary but don't be stupid."

I instantly looked back down to the tree and Yanni was nowhere to be found. Once again she had dipped off and left me hanging. She just sealed her fate this time she might as well just stay away from me because I wasn't dealing with her anymore.

I sat on the stoop massaging my swollen lip and bruised ego...

"Try to creep me, What I think that nigga sleepy"

DMX "How's It Going Down"

CHAPTER 15: DOWN WITH THE KING

The Homecoming Game was hype as ever! My whole family came out to cheer me on. I felt like I was right where I belonged beneath the bright lights with all eyes on me. Of course my grandmother had my attire on stunt mode. My hair was done and I was feeling like that girl for real. It felt good to look up in the stands and see all my people rooting for me. It was something different, I could get used to life outside the manor.

It was a great night for the Woo Babies. Chris showed off on the field, there was nothing the opposing team could do with him. The boy was out cold and they couldn't keep up. You would have thought he was playing against midget league kids the way he dominated through the defense. My grandfather suffered from severe back pain but he had no problem hopping up every time Chris got his hands on the ball. He led the Stonewall Jackson Generals to a 52-11 victory. The crowd went wild as the clock ran out and Chris danced around the field with his teammates.

"Run me that money I told you the kid was going to handle it on and off the field"

I turned around to see Zeke, grab some money out of Trey's hand. Trey was standing in the bleachers looking like he caught the vapors. He was shaking his head at the scoreboard still in disbelief that young Chris had that much talent. He should have known to never bet against the home team.

The lights from the football field had Trey glowing, his complexion was reminiscent of a golden sunset, the Multicolored Coogi hoodie he had on accentuated his fly.

A drop of rain landed on my arm snapped me back to reality. I looked up to the sky preparing to make a run for it, my hair had to last a couple more days. I wasn't taking any chances. The sky was clear as ever with no clouds in sight.

I didn't feel any more rain sprinkles either.

I looked back up at Trey and he was smiling a big stupid Kool-Aid smile at me. He wiped the side of his mouth and looked at me. Still smiling he pointed at me.

I put my hand up to my mouth and felt nothing but slobber.

Oh My God!

I drooled while staring at this boy, not only in public, but he watched me do it. Now I was going to have to change my name and move to somewhere nobody would recognize my face. As embarrassing as it was I just smiled at him and turned back around. My back was stiff as hell; I was trying to listen to see if he was telling any of his friends that I was slobbering at the sight of him. They went back to talking about the bet he lost and no mention of my saliva was ever made. Zeke said something about tonight being the last L he would ever take. I stopped listening and focused on smiling for pictures with my family in the stands.

The walk to the car was never ending, my grandmother had to stop and speak to everyone which would turn into mini reunion, and my grandfather had to dap up and hug the same people he would see tomorrow in the manor. I was just trying to get to the car, so I wouldn't have to face Trey on the way out.

"Mr. John your boy was tap dancing on the field"

Yep my back froze at the sound of that voice.

I didn't have to turn around to know this was becoming pure comedy.

My Granddaddy turned around and put his arm around Trey's shoulder. The two walked at a matched pace before any other words were spoken.

"He is the king of the field regardless of crowns him! Yeah he reminded me of somebody else. You know it's never too late to stop being hard headed and head hard towards your destiny." He took the Pittsburgh hat off of Treys head and put it on his own. "You must have known better than to run up on me with this on. What ya'll kids say these days, you got got!" He patted Trey on the back and pushed him forward, dismissing him to start a conversation with Zeke, Tyrell and Manny.

Trey looked at me grinning, "All kinds of people fell back there"

Half confused, "Back where"

He pointed back to the stands, "They slid in that puddle you left behind."

I couldn't help it I rolled my eyes whiled laughing.

I laughed all the way to car. He went on down the parking lot towards Zeke's Camaro and I couldn't help but to notice the breeze was perfect.

His phone rang and he yelled out to Zeke, "Yo we gotta dip Asap! They all flew past us hopped in the car and peeled out. I looked back at my grandfather who had stopped to talked to someone else and this time I didn't mind.

"And suddenly the ghetto didn't seem so tough

And though we had it rough, we always had enough"

Keep Your Head Up -2Pac

CHAPTER 16: READY TO DIE

When we arrived back to the manor, the place was swarming with five O. And the entire neighborhood was out, standing around whispering. The cops were rushing to yellow tape the crime scene but the crowd was closing in. Something had gone down in the back hallway of building 208 on Bowman Court. There were hushed conversations running through the crowd of who it might be. But none of the conversations offered any legitimate confirmation of who actually took their last breath in that pissy stairwell.

I spotted Ace, Tonika, Londa, Ronnie and Yanni all standing under a tree in deep conversation. I made my way through the agitated crowd to link up with them.

"What happened," I asked, hoping somebody could come through with the 411.

"Girl" was all Tonika could get out before all hell broke loose.

The coroner had pulled up and it was time to bring the bodies out, but the crowd would not back up. The police officers were yelling at the growing crowd of people, but nobody was budging. Finally, a path was cleared, and the first gurney came out. The crowd's reaction to Juan's body being wheeled to a vehicle was full of mixed emotions. His character wasn't exactly upstanding so there were a few "that's what that nigga gets" being tossed around.

"Somebody finally caught the neighborhood Jack boy slipping," Ace said.

"What are you talking about." Tonika pressed for more info, staring a hole into him as if that would speed up the process. I just rolled my eyes, everybody knew Ace took his time with everything he did. Juan would be buried before Ace finished the story. If he even started it, he ran with the big boys sometimes so getting him to speak on certain stuff with us was a tossup. Just as I expected Ace waved her off. He must have said too much already. Tonika pushed him and he slapped at the air in front of her. She grabbed him by the shirt and he tripped her. Only these two would get into a pushing match in the midst of a crime scene. There was movement in the crowd that made us refocus on the path that was constructed for the gurneys. It seemed as if the second gurney was coming down the pathway in slow motion.

There was no indication of who was under that sheet, the crowd was highly agitated at the unknown. All you could see was the person's shoes, we moved closer to get a more accurate look. My heart stopped beating.

I felt instantly sick, it was a silent hurt, a new form of pain that I was unsure of how to deal with at that time.

I felt my eyes fill up, and the tears slid down slowly. Just as slowly as the leg slid off the gurney revealing a crispy white shell toe, with a butterfly ankle bracelet.

Nooooooooooooooooooooooooooooooooooooooooooooooooooooooooo ooooooooooooooooo!!

This could not be right; this could not be life right now. The world could not be this cruel. My head was throbbing; my stomach was in knots.

I wanted my Mama, my grand mom, my Granddaddy, somebody to hold me. Because I was scared, who kills kids? Especially one so innocent and special.

My chest was tight.

My face was soaked.

My homecoming dress was dusty from being against the tree, and my heart was wounded.

When the word got through the crowd, of who was under that

second sheet, tensions rose to a whole new level. Nobody wanted to picture that reality as truth. A car pulled up and Mrs. Bernadette got out in her hotel work clothes. Nobody said anything, as she tried to process the scene, but you could tell she had no idea what was going on.

Ms. Irene, a sweet older lady, went over to her and asked her to call her sons. She looked at the tape and over to her apartment. She mumbled something about checking on Shay and her nephew first. Ms. Irene grabbed her hand as a police officer approached her, a few short seconds later, she screamed out for Jesus in such a piercing manner, I expected the sky to open up at that moment and the Lord to come down. I knew only God could ease her pain. Ms. Irene rocked her backed and forth, patted her back through all the sobs and wails, and prayed for her peace in her ear.

The scene was surreal; the crowd was heartbroken. All Shayla did was smile. She didn't bother anybody, she didn't deserve none of this.

My chest was now empty.

I had no feeling.

"JESUSSSSSSSSSSSSSSSSSSSSSSSSSSSSSSS! Not my baby! NOT MY BUTTERFLY! GET THEE BEHIND SATAN!!!! I REBUKE YOU I REBUKE YOU I REBUKE YOU!!!!!NOOOOOOOOOOOOOOOOOOOOOOOOOOOOOOOOOOOOOOOO OOOOOOOOOOO."

Mrs. Bernadette's pleading, caused so many tears to fall throughout the crowd. I'm sure every parent out there felt her despair. I bet a million tears hit the pavement that night and none of them would be enough to wash away the pain of this day. You could look in her face and see her heart was bleeding. She lifted her head up slowly to the heavens, I assumed she was bargaining with God, offering whatever it would take to bring her baby back. She sat down on the curb, in defeat and put her face in the palm of her hands, continuing to sob uncontrollably with the women of the neighborhood surrounding her and massaging her back.

A Cadillac sedan pulled up, a man hopped out and ran over to the crime scene yelling "Where is she? Where is my butterfly?" Mrs. Bernadette got up off the curb, approached the man with a stern look on her face.

"She is gone."

"What the fuck you mean she is gone."

"There was a shooting she was caught in the middle." Her voice was weak.

"Who the fuck shot my baby! And where the fuck where you!"

The crowd gasped in disbelief.

"I was at work, where I am everyday providing for mine. This is where I can afford to live remember. You sold our house and went to live with the girl you had been sneaking around with! Remember you told me that you would take care of Shayla and Daniel but that's it. Well I guess we both failed."

"Oh so this is my fault, How dare-?"

Holding her hand in his face and cutting him off, "Your words not mine, you have some of your children living up in a six-bedroom house overlooking the city, while my two are here making the best of what they have. Marcus plays your role and he shouldn't have to. You're living room is the size of my whole apartment. Some of your kids have cars, while I have to catch two buses for a ride to work. So maybe it takes me a little longer to get back and forth than the average person but I do what I have to provide for mine. With or without your inconsistent help."

"I don't show favoritism to my kids, I try to be there for all them."

"When is the last time you spoke to Daniel, and why haven't you yet to ask where he is amidst all this madness?"

He couldn't answer her or was too ashamed to. Either or he kept his mouth shut.

"Let me give you a little warning so this doesn't happen again, and you're not right back standing here!"

Pointing at the hallway, where Shayla took her last breath she spoke as if her mouth laced her next words with venom.

"You better keep a really good eye on what your other daughter is over here doing. See, if you talked to Daniel a little more maybe you'd know what was going on. Maybe he could put you up on game because all these children are doing is getting trapped because of the sins of their FATHER!"

She looked at him in disgust. "Now get out of my way."

She walked the slow, silent walk back to her apartment leaving him looking real vulnerable to a crowd of spectators that were judging him harshly at the current moment. He walked back over to his car, but he didn't pull off he just leaned up against it, staring at the hallway.

The news crews showed up trying to get an interview out of anybody that was willing to shed some lights on the horrific tragedy, but their efforts were unsuccessful. There was a code in this community pertaining to family business and somebody murmured that this is exactly what this was. I was confused by the statement, but I was too hurt to try and figure it out.

I looked up at the sky, and my mind drew a blank. I was raised not to question but my heart did not want to accept this. Cold world, Juan was out here robbing dudes of their profits, and young girls of their innocence. Shayla was just a casualty of the game.

"A ghetto love is the law that we live by

Day by day I wonder why my shorty had to die

I reminisce over my ghetto princess everyday"

"Renee" LOST BOYS

CHAPTER 17: LIFESTYLES OV DA POOR AND DANGEROUS

My grandmother came over to where we were standing, shook her head and instructed my friends to go home. Wrapping her arm around me, we heading back to her building in silence.

Neither of us spoke, I'm not even sure we would be able to in the first place.

I peeled off my homecoming attire and turned the shower to the hottest setting possible, I climbed in and cried until I was sure there wasn't a tear in me left. Once I had my pajamas on I went to the living room and laid on the couch. Grabbing my book bag, I took my notebook out and put my thoughts on paper.

He said he love you cause he different, little girl he lying

Tell him your heart dead broke so what he selling you aint buying

And if he aint offer nothing new you aint trying

He looking at you like everything you said is flying

over his head implying

That he's not used to get turned down

So walk away and don't turn around

Save yourself the heartache and the drama

Don't blame him blame his daddy he was raised by his mama

So he doesn't know that girls are more than objects

More than emotions more than drama

We could go on and on and on with no comma

But point blank period

When you get that women's intuition tell him you're not hearing it

Then when you diss him if he disrespects you

Automatic indication that you made the right choice

Don't say nothing back don't raise your voice

Don't waste your breathe on grown men with the soul of little boys

Silent goodbyes are the most heartfelt

I know you missing your father so any man will do

But don't take everything that somebody hands to you

As simple as Eve and the apple understand the truth

That everything that sounds good really isn't

Look deep down and find what's hidden

That you better off alone you can hold your own

You got whole life ahead to find out how it feels to be grown

If they can't love you right, then let them go on

When the smiles to frowns and the lows seem perplexing

Chuck the deuces and tell em to quit flexing

Aint no point of letting bad get worse

Wipe your eyes hold your head even if hurts

Cause aint nobody more important than me

that's what I told her

And when I winked in the mirror

She winked backed at me

      I flipped back the picture Shayla had drawn from and just stared. Soon as I put my pencil down, my uncle Plush was pushing Vina through the door. He had a death grip on her arm, of course she was being her usual self-jerking away and running her mouth recklessly. My grandmother came out the kitchen just in time to witness her youngest son send her daughter flying halfway across the room.

      "The streets are on fire tonight and this dummy want to be in the midst of the action." He smacked my grandmother's vase off the brass and glass leaf coffee table. It landed on the floor but didn't shatter.

      "I know you better pick my stuff up Melvin." She threw her hand up in the air. "Joe come and get your kids, because I will hurt one of them tonight."

      Turning back to Vina he barked in her face "Dudes lost their sister, their little cousin out there tonight, isn't no love being shown out there. Use what's left of your brain and chill for one damn night."

      Plush was a short, stocky, dark skinned version of my Granddaddy. Where my Granddaddy was calm and gentle, plush was the flip side times ten. My Granddaddy talked with his hands to get you to understand where he was coming from. Plush talked with his fist to make you feel where he was coming from. He picked the vase up before he even noticed that I was laying on the couch. His whole demeanor softened as soon as we made eye contact.

      "Lil lady you looked so pretty out there tonight, Unc was real proud."

      "You came!" now this was a complete shocker, Plush didn't like large crowds and barely went anywhere outside of his comfort zone.

      He smirked "Lil Lady I wasn't going to miss that for nothing. I didn't come in but I watched it all from the fence. And you were out there shining baby."

That's when the realization hit me that Vina was not there. My aunt Elliana, who was my mother's older sister even made it. She was letting me have a slumber up her house to celebrate next weekend. I needed to figure who all I was going to invite as well.

I rolled my eyes at my aunt, Vina who I saw everyday not showing up made me feel some type of way.

"Why you didn't you come RaVina Camille," I asked with enough aggression to make the whole house go quiet. The fact that I said her whole name brought my grandfather who I'm sure was already eavesdropping of out his bedroom.

"Joe you have some nerves, I call you when Tom and Jerry going at it and you don't respond, but soon as Era open her mouth you come flying out the back. Now don't be concerned now you should have been concerned when your son was smacking vases all over the place. Almost missed my foot."

"Ma, you so daggone dramatic. That vase was nowhere near you. And I smacked one vase which I picked up."

"RAVINA, WHY DID YOU NOT COME!"

She dismissed my question with a wave of her hand. My feelings had been hurt enough for one day so I let it go.

My grandfather slid over to the couch, patted the top of my head, threw a fake jab at Plush, then embraced him in a tight hug. He stepped back laughing at his sons rugged haircut.

"Boy do you own a brush"

"Just because you sit in the window brushing and greasing your hair all day long don't mean I'm about that life. Who you think you are Eddie Kane?"

My grandfather chuckled "watch that mouth I still got it young man!"

Plush looked over at Vina, "you need to keep an eye on that one she about to be lost in the sauce. I bet tonight be the last time, she ever bucks at me in the street and don't catch one"

He snatched a pillow off the couch and sent it flying at head, she ducked just in time, but with the look he gave her he might as well have connected. He went in the kitchen to kiss my grandmother, and disappeared back out the door into the night.

The door opened back up and Plush ran back over to the couch and where Vina was and ran her pockets. Nobody moved until he was finished. Whatever he was looking for he didn't find. He just nodded his head and went on out the door.

My grandfather busted out laughing, he shook his head at her and said "I think it's best you don't go out that front door for the next couple days under no circumstances. You hear me."

She rolled her eyes.

He looked at her daring her to do it again. She didn't.

"You looked real pretty, out there tonight. Honey I proud of you. Now I'm sorry about your little friend but you try to get some rest ok."

I just needed for this day to hurry up and be over. I closed my eyes and tried to get some rest but all I could see was that one Adidas tennis shoe and the butterfly ankle bracelet. I stayed up all night being haunted by Shayla's wardrobe. I was drained, I didn't even have the energy to tell on Vina, when she went out the back door.

The next day the manor was a zoo, it was full of reporters and police officers. The story made the front of the newspaper, **Murder and Mayhem in the Manor: 16-year-old Girl Killed.** I read the article and became sick to my stomach they made it seem as if Shayla was Juan's girlfriend and it was a drug deal gone bad. I guess that's the best they could come up with since nobody was talking to the police or the news. But according to the conversation that was taking place on my grandmother's stoop, the streets had launched their own investigation and the findings were damn right disturbing.

Mrs. Taylor who lived across the hall from Juan's mama said she heard the commotion in the back hallway. Whoever ran up in the hallway on Juan, did not intend for Shayla to come down the steps behind him. She said after the shots rang out, they just kept screaming "Damn! Damn! Damn! Damn!"

She started to say something else, but thought better of it. Her silence spoke volumes. *She knew who did it.*

It was written all over her face. My people watching skills, allowed me to analyze body language. Whatever she witnessed or heard was weighing heavily on her heart. But she knew what the consequences of sharing it with the wrong person could be.

"Anybody seen Bernadette's boys? I know they are taking this really hard. They looked over that girl so thoroughly I know they are going crazy that something like this happened." Ronnie's mother was shaking her head as she asked the question aloud that most were pondering over silently.

When she posed her last question, Mrs. Taylor's body stiffened. I could have sworn she was holding her breath. She covered her mouth with her left hand, but that didn't stop the vomit from coming up and spilling out on to the porch. My grandmother hopped up to come to her friend's aid. Whatever that woman was holding on to, the mere thought of it just made her instantly sick to her stomach.

"God is who we praise, even though the Devil's all up in my face"

Bone Thugs N Harmony "Crossroads"

CHAPTER 18: HOUSE OF PAIN

A few hours later, my grandmother had prepared several dishes to take to Mrs. Bernadette's apartment. Her and a few other ladies had made enough food so the family wouldn't have to worry about cooking while they mourned the loss of Shayla. I helped my granny carry the stuff down the street, as we walked past the crime scene, an instant chill ran through my body, the 90-degree weather couldn't even add any warmth, it was bone deep. The hallway was still taped up; the officers were gone but the news was posted outside trying to get a story out of anyone who was willing to talk.

The 12 o'clock news story was a generic run of the events with no real interview but the neighborhood would get a shock come six o'clock. I watched the reporter give Ray a pack of cigarettes and then prep him with a microphone. Now this was about to get real interesting because Ray was always around and who knows what he actually knew or saw, but one thing for sure he wouldn't hesitate to say it if he was drunk or high. And it was seldom that he wasn't. My grandmother looked at me and blurted out "This is going to be a hot ass mess. "I nodded my head in agreement. "A hot ass mess" she said again as if I didn't hear her the first time.

To my surprise Mrs. Bernadette's apartment was popping, people from all over the neighborhood had brought food and she was sitting on the couch seeming to be in better spirits. Her sons were nowhere to be found again, and she wasn't volunteering any information as to their whereabouts either. It was something not being said here and I couldn't put my finger on it. The apartment was nice and clean. Her living was decorated in black and gold, there were a lot of nice African pictures adorning the walls. I wanted to go see Shayla's room but I didn't want to pry I just wondered if she had any drawings of her own on her walls. She really was talented.

The door opened up and Marcus walked in alone, Mrs. Bernadette got up and ran to her oldest son and lost all of her composure. He stood strong and firm, holding on to his mother as if letting her go would break her. They stayed in that sorrowful embrace for at least five minutes. The whole mood of the room completely changed, and the sadness from yesterday succumbed the entire mental state of everyone in close proximity. Tissues were being passed around, as this mothers sobs were being soothed by her son.

"I worked two jobs to make sure you kids had what you needed," she moaned, "but what you needed was me here." I guess her ex-husbands words had gotten to her yesterday making her feel guilty about her daughter's death.

Marcus was not trying to hear it at all.

He looked her dead in her face "nah you can't blame yourself for this one, it's on us!"

He walked her over to the couch and walked back out the door, with a look in his eyes that anybody outside of that door should be leery of.

We stayed for a little bit longer and made it home just in time for the six o'clock news. The manor flashed across the screen along with a picture of Shayla looking angelic in a pink dress. The headline said *Teenage Girl Gunned Down in Hallway in City Project.*

The reporter appeared on the screen with an eager expression about the exclusive interview he had scored with Ray.

Ray appeared, his bald head was shining due to the sweat that had mounted there. His sunken in face showed a hint of how handsome he used to be. The years of alcohol abuse and drug use had taken a toll on his once meticulous appearance. He opened his mouth to showcase a set of perfect pearly white teeth, and a smile that hardly ever appeared on the streets I encountered him in.

"I have with me here Mr. Ray Reynolds, he's going to shed some light on the tragic events that took place here yesterday in the Orchard

Manor projects located here on the cities West Sider, where a young girl and a 23-year-old man where gunned down inside of a building stairwell around 10pm."

The reporter turned around to point in the direction of the crime scene and then turned back around to introduce Ray.

"Mr. Reynolds what can you tell us about the situation that unfolded in your community yesterday."

Ray rubbed the sweat off of his forehead and said, "Well."

My grandfather sat up in the mauve recliner, pointed the remote at the screen and turned the volume up.

"Well,"

My grandmother leaned forward. "Aw shit now!"

Ray looked at the reporter and pointed his finger.

"We have been over here alone, all this time and the only time the city wants to come through here is when it's something negative going on. These kids out here organize their own kickball tournaments, basketball games, dance routines, and whatever else to pass the time in these trenches. This community has block parties, cookouts and we do it without the cities help. Now we have a tragedy on our hands and we didn't ask for the cities help but now Charleston is concerned. Where is your concern on a daily basis? Don't try to come get a story off our pain, a young girl is dead, a community is mourning and you guys want to watch so you can pass judgement! When any other day of the week you ride pass these buildings with no concern for our lives. So on behalf of the people of Orchard Manor I want to tell you and whoever else to Mind Ya Business!"

The young reported knew he struck gold with interviewer. I swear a cheer erupted through every apartment in every building. My grandfather leaned back in his recliner and laughed and shook his head,

"Boy oh Boy Ray told them mind their damn business"

      I had a new found respect for Ray, sometimes it's not the messenger it's the message.

And he delivered full force with that one. "Mind ya Business"

Getting my trusty notebook out I began writing

Could've grown up to be a menace to society.

but I chose to start the revolution quietly

for the Pac inside of

me let em judge the book by the cover

mentally equivalent to a Louisville slugger

respect the hustle but don't underestimate the struggle

But if I don't talk about haters and the club they won't feel me

if I dumb down my intellect it's not the real me

so should I conceal me

until they catch on to the bigger picture

reality and ignorance is quite a mixture

So I'm at a crossroads between knowing and not growing

I'm due but not showing

my delivery ain't ready

the anticipation got me breathing heavy

for the Katrina in my soul can't withstand the levy

but the boys on my block to busy painting their Chevy's

My heart is tatted with my homies that didn't make it

with this the despair of the fiends that could not shake it

and the teenage mothers in the cycle that could not break it

the deadbeat daddies the role of fatherhood that would not take it

If you think that's despair you are mistaking

surviving and reviving what's left into what's next

giving up has never been a reflex

profiled into one of the usual suspects

I know the routine quite well

long as you try you can never fail

Don't breathe the bull shit just exhale

Let a Ray of sunshine come through before you inhale

You won't judge my testimony so no I won't be your witness

Do like you been doing and mind your business!

I looked up at my grandfather still smiling, from Ray standing up for the neighborhood. My grandfather mumbled something about "family business" I wouldn't understand until Chris came back for his Fila's the following night.

"Now I see the importance of history

Why my people be in the mess that they be

Many journeys to freedom made in vain

By brothers on the corner playin' ghetto games

I ask you, Lord why you enlightened me

Without the enlightenment of all my folks

He said, cuz I set myself on a quest for truth"

"TENNESSEE" ARRESTED DEVELOPMENT

CHAPTER 19: THE INFAMOUS

I was in my uncle's room playing Duck Hunt, trying to release some steam off on these birds. My aim was impeccable. A knock on the door startled me.

"Come in" I yelled still focused on the screen.

"Come on baby girl, you know you can't see me with the chopper,"

"It's E THUGGA get it right, I'm not missing nothing."

"You talk really good with your square self," he said laughing at his own joke because I for sure wasn't. "Listening to Bone isn't going to put no type of G in your heart!"

"What do you want stranger, you start scoring touchdowns and stuff, and I don't even recognize you. Used to be my homie you used to be my ace now I want to slap the taste out your mouth, matter of fact get out my grandma house!"

We both laughed at my impromptu freestyle. He came back at me "I know you peep the sound, it's the lords on the block." He started laughing at me and knocking on the window as a reminder.

"What do you want fool"

"I need my Fila's I got to pay the rent up for the rest of the year. I already know you ran through some dollars I hope you didn't put too much of a dent in there."

"Huh, ain't nobody gonna buy them shoes off of you, they came out six months ago. That's not going to help the rent," then it dawned on me. He was about to put his Hi Tecs back on. Although we never talked about it, I knew he was the one who got ole boy that night.

"Get my shoes nosey, you worse than your grandmother yo!"

"I'm telling her you said that"

"And I'm telling her how you really put in work with those Jordan's at the flat top."

I pointed the orange Nintendo gun at him. "Snitches get....."

He smiled, "you might actually be cut from the same cloth"

We both laughed, but then I got serious, "Is that why nobody won't tell what happened to Shayla?"

A look of disgust crept across his face he knew I caught it and he couldn't hide it.

"Nah that was just crazy the way that situation played out. Juan's time was coming, he was on legit bullshit, Marcus was just trying to protect his family."

"What are you talking about?"

He walked over to the door and opened it to make sure my grandparents were still in the living room. He closed it and must have been debating on if he was going to finish the story or not. I stomped my foot.

"Daniel was getting high with Juan and taking Shayla to the crib with him when he did it. When Marcus found out her snapped. Shayla was 16 and Daniel was 17 so he felt responsible. Daniel was stealing from him to cop from Juan, while he was getting high Juan was taking advantage of Shayla. After the fight the day on the court, Daniel tried to get back on Juan's good side because he knew his secret addiction and Juan was his only supplier. Nobody else would be crazy enough to violate that family like that. Juan was on some cutthroat shit, so he told him to bring his sister but this time he said she couldn't leave. Daniel had to come back for her. They got into a scuffle, the little cousin had come looking for them, heard the arguing and went and got Marcus. Marcus went the backway because the door gets stuck and doesn't lock,

97

same time Juan comes out the hallway and Marcus catches him with a couple and they hit Shayla who was running out the back door behind him. Marcus wouldn't leave Shana, so dudes had to literally dragged him up out of the hallway. It was painful to watch, that's why nobody's talking. That was never meant for her, and her brothers got to live with that every day that's punishment enough. Juan been running around her real reckless, robbing folks and plotting his day was coming."

That was too much for me to process.

Daniel smoking crack. Juan molesting Shayla...Marcus killing them both...Mind Ya Business.

Now I understood why nobody was curious as to where the sons were. The awkward conversation between Mrs. Bernadette and Marcus...." This one on us Ma, don't blame yourself"

Knowing the truth didn't make me feel any better. It made me feel even more hopeless. How could this be real, how can you live with that type of pain hanging over your heart.

I went to the closet dug in the back corner and pulled out his Fila's. They still looked crispy, so maybe he could sell them for some rent money. He took the shoes out of my hands sat down on the bed, and pulled two socks out. Both socks contained nothing but hundred dollar bills, Big Faces. He counted the money meticulously, three times to be exact. He looked at me, confused "it's all here."

"I didn't go through your stuff."

He just stood there looking stupid. "It's been months and you never touched nothing. I can't leave nothing at home for five minutes and it's a wrap."

He peeled of a hundred and gave it to me. I stared at it, for a whole ten minutes. I had never had a whole hundred-dollar bill to myself. I was about to walk straight to Hills Department Store and get a whole bunch of books and magazines. I asked him did he want to join me on my literary expedition.

He chuckled, "E, you are crazy one of kind, I put you on to some real life gangster

shit, you go through it internally, then you bounce back and want to go buy some fairytales with the cash I had to get out of the mud. I love it though, don't let the world have your heart it's one of kind."

I kind of got him but I was really already spending this Hundo in my head to let it sink in.

"Let me go grab this money order so I can pay this rent before 5."

"How is your mom doing these days, I never see her out anymore."

His next sentence struck a major nerve with me, one I wouldn't be able to shake.

"She lost in the sauce"

"Used to get high just to get by used to have to puff my L

In the morning before I get fly

I ate something a couple of forties made me hate somethin'

I did some coke now I'm ready to take something"

"Slippin" DMX

CHAPTER 20: THE MISEDUCATION

After the Shayla's death, I was basically on home confinement. I couldn't go anywhere; my grandmother was cautious about the growing turmoil that was brewing in the neighborhood. I was content, the weather was changing and I never was a fan of the cooler seasons. My mom had to work early in the morning so I stayed at my grandparents' house more often. I was still doing well in school, and my book collection was growing. The library at school became my friend. I often sat on the porch after school with a new book and read while expanding my people watching skills. Jasmine finally had her mystery baby, and she walked past every day going to catch the bus to the local college. One day she stopped in front of the stoop and said, "do you ever stop reading?" I laughed and told her I wasn't allowed to; this was my escape from my reality.

"Girl I feel you on that, I'm determine to get my degree so I can get me and my baby out of here. Hopefully I will be finished next May and I can dip up out of this place."

"What are you going to school for"

"I want to be a psychiatrist; you know half my family crazy."

We both laughed because I knew she was telling the truth. She waved bye making a dash for the city bus that was approaching quickly.

One day I was surprised to see her coming off the hill with the baby in a stroller looking frustrated and overwhelmed. She looked up at me as she reached the stoop.

"Hey lil girl, can't talk long today I gotta take Miya to school with me. My mom is having an episode and I just can't miss this class I have to give a presentation today. I'll fail if I don't make it. And I can't afford to lose my financial aid."

"Leave her here"

"Huh, you don't know how to watch a baby, do you?"

"My grandmother gets off work in fifteen minutes, she'll understand, plus I'm super bored. I know how to make bottles, change diapers and make babies laugh. She will be ok."

Looking at the bus stop, at me, then back at baby Miyah, she looked distraught and started fidgeting.

"I don't really know about this but taking her would be a hassle, I can give you three dollars for watching her."

The bus was coming over the bridge, she looked at me, pushed the stroller to the porch and ran up the street. The bus driver slowed up waiting for her and Mr. Todd to board.

As the bus went bye she was waving and smiling at Miya and I the whole time.

Once I got us in the house and settled, it was on. I built Miya a fort out of pillows on the pink carpeted floor, grabbed my stuffed animals out of the closet and prepared to play with her. Miya was such a happy baby, she laughed and smiled at me and it warmed my soul. She climbed up in my lap to kiss my cheeks and play with my eyelids. She didn't cry not once since her mother left. My grandmother came in the house flopping on the couch and closed her eyes.

Immediately Miya started babbling in baby talk.

My grandmother opened her eyes slowly and said "What in the world, who in the hell would leave you with their baby?"

"Jasmine didn't have a sitter, she had a presentation at college and she would have to take the baby on a 45-minute bus ride with her so I thought I would help her out."

"I don't know Jasmine that well but she tries hard to not to be like these other girls around here. She's determined to not let anything stop her, so I guess she really needed a sitter to leave her poor child here with you."

Miya crawled over to my Grandmother and reached up for her. My grandmother leaned down and picked her up. Miya was so beautiful, big brown soft curls framed her face, showcasing her almond shape light brown eyes. She was the perfect mixture of caramel and chocolate. Jasmine had given birth to a real live doll baby. She looked up at my grandmother and kissed her cheek, then laughed a baby laugh and after that my first night of babysitting was over.

My grandmother would not give her back.

She cooked with Miya in her arms, went on the porch with Mia in her arms and went to the corner store all without putting the baby down. When Jasmine got off the bus at ten she came directly to the house. Miya was in the recliner with my grandmother. She had been freshly bathed and was smelling just like Johnson's and Johnson's. My grandmother told Jasmine it was fried chicken in the kitchen if she wanted to eat. Jasmine ate in the kitchen then came back in the living room with us. She looked like she wanted to cry, "thank you, it's just me and Miya most of the time. This means a lot I just really appreciate this."

She started gathering the baby's things, my grandmother told her "I just bathed her, she doesn't need to go out in this night air. I'm off tomorrow so you can pick her up in the morning." She grabbed Miya and headed down the hallway to her bedroom.

Jasmine just shrugged her shoulders "Well I'm not going home either; my mom is probably still up there throwing dishes."

We laughed and then we both read our books until we fell asleep.

My grandmother came in the living fussing at me and Jasmine for sleeping on her new couches, Mia was on her hip fussing right along with her. Every time my grandmother open her mouth, Miya would open hers. It was so cute and funny. That's when I noticed it. Miya looked like my grandmother. Just a darker version

"Nanny, Miya looks like you with a tan."

My grandmother turned to look at Miya and her mouth dropped.

"Who's this child's father Jasmine"

Jasmine, frowned her face up at my granny and said "Your son"

My grandmother almost dropped the baby. I saw that vein come out of her forehead and thought maybe Jasmine better make a run for it.

"You mean to tell me this is my grandchild, and you didn't think to inform me such young lady."

Jasmine looked at my grandmother confused.

"Talk girl!"

"You said that it wasn't your responsibility to take care of Ryan's baby while he was jail, we made this baby and that's on us. And you weren't sure if it's his anyways I better go find the out of towner and pin it on him."

My grandmother looked at Jasmine like she was crazy. I know she said her family was, maybe she could be to.

"Girl I have never talked to you about this child, I never knew anything about this baby being of no relation to me. What are you talking about?"

"Vina told my mama that's what you said."

Vina was The Bride of Chucky I swear....

"RAVIIIIIIIIIIIIIIIIIIIIIINAAAAAAAAAAAAAAAAAA CAMILLE LYING ASS WALTERS GET IN HERE NOW!!!"

My Granddaddy came flying down the hallway, Vina came out of her room looking like last night's Blue Diamond special with mascara running down her face and puffy eyes. "WHAT!"

My grandmother walked over to her and poked her in the forehead.

"Now tell me when I said I wanted nothing to do with this baby, I wasn't taking care of Ryan's responsibilities, and she better find the father. VINAAA WHEN!" She said pounding her fist on the top of the television stand.

Vina looked as if she just noticed me and Jasmine were even in the living room.

"WHEN!"

Vina scratched her head and still didn't speak.

My grandfather was just sitting on the arm of the couch shaking his head. He had a hurt expression on his face. Miyah must have sensed it because she leaped from my grandmother's arms into his. She started smiling and playing with his beard and mustache causing him to laugh.

My grandmother looked like she wanted to smack Vina out of her daze.

"I'll tell you what I'm not going to do, that's cater to your grown unemployed ass, you are no longer my responsibility since you know so much I'm sure you will do just fine on your own."

Vina looked at me and Jasmine, rolled her eyes and went back in her bedroom. My grandfather was having so much fun with his new grandbaby that he didn't notice she was dumping his tobacco on the floor while he was bouncing her on his knee. My grandmother hollered when she noticed the mess Miya made. She yelled at me to get the dust pan and broom. Instantly I wasn't the princess of the castle anymore, Miya had turned me in to Cinderella.

Jasmine ended up moving into my uncle's room until her apartment was ready at the end of the month. She was relieved she didn't have to deal with anymore of her mother's psychotic episodes and she had a safe and reliable babysitter for Miya. Her and Vina did not speak at all, but Vina actually had a job now waitressing and she seemed a lot happier. She didn't even complain when Jasmine would tie up the phone lines all day arguing with the people at the Financial Aid office at State over her money. I got my notebook out and wrote one for Jasmine.

My diapers were Fendi

At the age of 13 I copped a light blue Bentley

Let me stop pretending

Cause right now Sallie Mae won't stop sending

me these letters but I think they should start extending

the date to never

will they see this cheddar?

I thought school was to make life better

not forever debtor

I guess I confused higher learning

With high earnings

Yeah right school should be free

How can the preparation for the future come with a fee?

Especially when most folks can't do a damn thing with their degree

Is it me or does it seem like a conspiracy

That the only way you can leave the bottom

is to hit the books

And financial aid seems like loan sharking crooks

I'd rather be a model student can I pay you with my looks

Cause my textbooks cost more than my rent

And my tuition is already spent

What is my teacher even talking about?

Let me read this myself and No Mrs. Philosopher

I don't need no help

I feel like you wasting my time and ruining my credit

I bet it never crossed your mind

That school is my last hope to reverse the cycle

I can't sing or ball like Michael

Affirmative action what does that mean, equally

I'm just trying to get some paper legally

So my younger cousins can see

That hard work pays off

And there is a better way

So can you please understand

That you can't get paid until I get paid

Did I complain when my disbursement was delayed

Yes, I did so mutual is what the feeling is

I grabbed my Walkman and pressed play on the new 2 PAC.

Now Brenda's gotta make her own way

Can't go to her family, they won't let her stay

No money no babysitter, she couldn't keep a job

She tried to sell crack, but end up getting robbed

"Brenda's Got A Baby" 2PAC

CHAPTER 21: IT WAS WRITTEN

It was 1999 and I was preparing to graduate from high school. I had a few scholarships to different colleges, but it seemed like WVU in Morgantown was as far as I would get away from the manor. In 8th grade I joined a program called Upward Bound it was for underprivileged kids who wanted to go to college. That was my motivation to be the first one in my family to graduate with a degree. So every Saturday I took the city bus to West Virginia State College to take college courses. The Director of the Program was the Mother Teresa of Trio Programs. I Mrs. Chaney was a true African Queen, she embodied everything women should be and I don't know if I could ever thank her enough for believing in me. She was an awesome mentor and I vowed to make her proud of me. I kept myself busy trying to not get caught up in the hood antics, not to mention I worked at a bookstore/coffee shop, all throughout high school. Once I turned 14 I made sure I had a job every summer, I wanted to make sure there was never a paper shortage because I was most definitely not a trust fund baby.

I was still quite the square chick as Chris usually referred to me as Squaresha. This used to be a major argument between us, the fact that I didn't drink or smoke and never had my cherry popped earned me that title. He said I should go ahead and be a nun. I thought I was a pretty girl and I liked my face, and I was a hundred percent sure my grandmother would break my face if she caught me doing anything other than what I was supposed to. I figured she had enough dealing with Vina, that girl was now a stone cold looney tune. Every time she came to visit it was something dramatic, she moved out and moved in with her new boyfriend. He was ugly too, all her boyfriends were ugly. That was probably her karma, she kept falling for ugly dudes because her attitude was ugly as hell. She was still mad at mad at me from the last time they came to visit. I told Miya to go in the living and do the new cheer I had just taught her. Every time I think about it my whole body gets weak. Miya went right in the living and starting stomping and clapping. She yelled in her voice that only Me and my grandmother could understand. "U-G-L-Y you don't have no alibi you ugly!" My grandmother tried to contain her laughter to the point, she was just sitting in her recliner with tears, rolling down her face. She kept acting like she didn't know what Miya was saying or the fact that I sent her in there to do it. Next thing you know Hasir comes in the house and picks right up on what she is saying. He picks her up and starts doing the cheer with her. By this time my grandmother is choking in the chair trying not to bust out laughing. Vina's dude is on the couch just looking evil and ugly for no reason. Finally, Vina catches on to the cheer and is like, "Damn do another one, cause aint nobody in here that ugly that ya'll have to keep repeating."

Her boyfriend snapped out of whatever he was thinking about and asked her. "Who Ugly."

My grandmother howled like a wolf. She completely lost it, she laughed so hard her back was shaking. She could not stop laughing.

"Mom it's not that funny,"

That's when I knew she was crazy, she was sitting up here with this ugly man and didn't know it.

So I tried to not stress my grandparents, and do the normal thing, because I know they had a hard time dealing with a son in jail, a daughter who was a nut case, and son who thought he was a WWE champion. The other two wasn't that bad, but with those three their heads and hands were full.

I was in advanced courses so most of my classmates were white, I developed a few friendships based on the familiarity of being around each other every day. I was invited to a couple of house parties with my friends from school and half the time I was amazed. These white honor roll students were literally in a class by their self, drinking beer, smoking weed, doing coke and sleeping with each other. I felt like I was watching a Vh1 special on the The Secret Life of Honor Society Students. I never indulged in the action I just watched and laughed like is this how The

Babysitters Club grew up. Actually it was low key confusing to me, most of these kids had everything they ever needed and wanted, huge homes, their own cars, allowances, credit cards, name brand clothing and these kids were getting high. The weed didn't bother me, I didn't even really view that as a drug, my grandfather puffed that exotic heavy, it took me years to realize that's what else he put in his pipe. It wasn't always just tobacco. He swore the Mary jane helped the sciatic nerve in his back. But the fact they were snorting lines blew my mind, being a dope fiend would never be the thing to do for me. I knew people who turned to drugs to escape the sad realism of what their life had become, to escape things that life had not prepared them for, to escape themselves. These kids were doing dope to be cool, what type of shit was that.

I was beyond baffled at how two different forms of the same drug affected communities differently. The kids I knew who fell victim to the era of the ready rock were in despair, lives damn near closed too ruined. Thinking back to all the ones who were dear to me that slipped to the other side, brought gloom to my mental state. After Shayla's death, her brother Daniel started freebasing heavy, he never could shake the habit. Every time I seen him walking around the manor, looking lost I think about how fly and fresh he used to be. I always wondered what happened to Trey's twin brother Tevin, well apparently he got strung out tried to steal money from their mother ending up beating her up really bad and has been in a mental hospital ever since. But the one that hurt me the most was Jasmine, because I knew how bad she wanted to break the cycle. Once she moved out of my grandmother's apartment and got her own place she went wild with that freedom. I guess she was tired of struggling so they turned her place into a cooking spot for the work, she ended up catching a conspiracy charge and is currently serving fifteen. My uncle came home two days before she went in, he has Miya and is doing the best he can to raise her right with the help of my grandparents. All these souls lost to crack, but these kids in here are living the life snorting cocaine without a worry in the world. They'll probably go to good colleges, get good jobs, get married and their drug usage will be labeled as experimenting as a youth. Meanwhile crack Is eradicating hope in three different generations in my neighborhood. My age group and below, we are the crack baby generation, developmental issues galore, ignored by society and looked down upon. Crackheads don't go to rehab; they go to prison. Mia will be 20 when Jasmine comes home, that hurts my heart every time I think about it. Her father missed her birth due to incarceration and her mother will be in the same situation, missing most of her childhood life. I hope she breaks the mold, because it's a hard battle to fight, when you've been systemically conditioned to believe that you're going to end up a statistic. 12th grade is when I developed that chip on my shoulder that would eventually turn into a boulder...

Anybody ever wonder what would happen if the sun didn't come up

Or is everybody to busy looking for a come up

This aint about you

don't interrupt my interview

This is strictly my inner views

My struggle is 360 degrees from the church pews

To the cranberry and grey goose

To the verbal abuse of having a short fuse

Changing my mind like I change my hairdo's

Never admit that I'm torn so I'd rather play confused

I refuse to excuse those that don't walk in my shoes

But think they can handle these stilettos

I am damn proud of my struggle hand me my medals

The rose that grew from concrete

With a thorn in every petal

Feeling like I should be further

But I chose to settle

Like the pot calling the kettle

Black but replacing it with wack

But I'm not dope enough

I used to be raw but now I'm getting stepped on

Insomnia just to avoid getting slept on

Wanted to cause some ruckus but instead I crept on

Choosing my battles wisely never been impressed with icy

Prefer the conversation to flow quite nicely

But rare for folks to captivate my blank stare

I guess I'm crazy cause I'm not all there

Part of me is stuck in bricks where I was born

Part of me refusing to conform

with what is consistent with the norm

Don't take my word for it we all have been misinformed

The American Dream is not the same for everybody

A cross between Gandhi and Gotti

The bottom looking at the top Beam me up Scotty

What are we fighting for windmill, taekwondo, karate?

The war starts within

And if you aint right there, how you gonna win?

How you gonna win when you aint right within...Ask Lauryn

CHAPTER 22: ONLY GOD CAN JUDGE ME

Senioritis hit me hard in March, everything bored me and I couldn't wait to start my new journey as a college student. I just really wanted to go to the movies and talk on the phone all night. I had a few crushes here and there but still didn't have a serious boyfriend yet, and I didn't think I wanted one either. Most of the guys at school couldn't relate to me and I truly believed their thought process was somewhat juvenile. They were at school arguing over sports, battling over video games, when I knew dudes who were paying bills at 13. But then again it wasn't their fault they were allowed to have a normal childhood. It would take me years to realize I was only attracted to guys who were broken like me. Because I was quiet, well-mannered and well spoken, folks assumed that I was the traditional impoverished kid just trying to make it out of the ghetto. In reality I wanted to take the ghetto with me, I believed my whole hood deserved better. I never wanted to truly leave I just wanted to elevate it.

My sheltered life was coming to an end, because I know longer asked to do things, I just did them, I had my own money so that was a plus. I never did anything crazy so my family didn't question my comings and goings. There was a club on the west side that a few of my friends from school would attend, they didn't really care how old you were as long as you paid the cover charge to get in. Club Vertigo was the place to be according to chatter at the lunch tables. They used to try and talk me into going but I couldn't muster up the courage to step foot in there. I used to joke with my friends that I was going to Club Vertigo to find me a boyfriend. I was infatuated with Bone Thugs N Harmony and Allen Iverson, so I should have already known my preference in guys was a little more on the rugged side.

"Y'all should have come last night it was some fine dudes in there from the East Side." Layla was squeezing her hands together like she was having a moment enjoying the flash back.

We all laughed because she was always extra at the lunch table.

Layla Hall was out of her mind, she was an extremely pretty caramel complected, box braid wearing, too thick to be in 11th grade cutie who stirred up shit everywhere she went. She was just a trouble maker and didn't care. Her family had moved to the manor two years ago and she thought she was the Queen of her Court. We just let her talk because she could argue for days and not care if she was making sense or not. All she would say was "Like I said" over and over again, but not ever really say anything. She was crazy and funny at the same time, but she was a major flirt and actually had the nerve to get mad if a guy didn't entertain her flirting.

Chris came over to the table to ask us if one of us would braid his little brother's hair after school. Of course Layla was all for it.

Frowning his face up and totally ignoring her, "Kallie can you do it like you did Mrs. Porters granddaughters?"

Kallie shook her head, "nah I got detention for the rest of the week for skipping gym"

The whole table looked at her like she was crazy.

Laughing hysterically Monie told her, "you for sure slow of all the classes to skip why would you skip gym"

Kallie's eyes got real heavy.

She took a deep breath and then spazzed.

"I could give a fuck what y'all think. Y'all always laughing at shit like it's sweet. My grandmother takes care of all of us, since my mama ran off and the only thing that make her happy is watching the Young and The Restless."

She pointed her finger at the whole table.

"Now you bitches and bitch boys can laugh all you want but so what I skipped gym to watch the soaps in the teachers' lounge so I could tell my grandmother what happened until the cable got cut back on"

She grabbed her book bag, gave us all the finger and headed back in the direction of the teachers' lounge.

We fell out laughing. Kallie wore her heart on her sleeve, but she wasn't weak at all. She was emotional as hell. She cursed us out at least once a month. This was mild in comparison to her usual rants.

"The soap opera skipper" Layla was about to get started, she was always ready to clown when it came down to it. "Her dramatic ass could have gotten an Emmy for the best lunchtime performance for that act she just pulled."

Missy shook her head "knock it off Layla that is some real shit right there, that's loyalty there she just returning the love she gets from her grandmother. Maybe that's all she can give her right now. It might be small but in reality that shit big. I bet Mrs. Rosa be hype as hell to hear what Kayla has to say when she gets home."

Chris nodded his head in agreement "I Overstand her, I'll skip, hop jump over any obstacle to bring a smile to one of mine face."

Licking her lips, Layla stated flirtatiously "you can jump on me," putting her hands on her thick hips she smiled.

He looked at her, tired of throwing herself at him when he was trying to handle business. "Your ass fat but your mind shallow."

Ouch!!!

Aw shit...

Why would he even get her started? Now she was about to do a show.

Waving her arms like a bird in distress she got aggressive with her tone, "I never paid attention to what a broke nigga thought of me."

Chris shrugged his shoulders, "until you can keep a nigga attention you don't have to worry about me ever thinking of you."

"Get your money up. I get all the attention I need enough to last me for years."

He laughed, "let's not do this ok, you'll be fat in four years. You know it too that's why you always SKIPPING lunch"

I think the whole cafeteria went quiet at this point. Layla was notorious for arguing with people until the fat lady sang, but it was quite obvious Chris was not to be played with today and he was on a mission to shut her up.

"You got me fucked up, this body is a brick house and I'm going to stay naturally blessed. You might run shit on the field but you going to watch how you run your mouth to me, broke ass!!!"

"Isn't nothing natural about your body, it's those hormones from the birth control blowing your ass up, you wouldn't need if it all these niggas wasn't running up in you."

"LIKE I SAID, LIKE I SAID, LIKE I SAID, LIKE I SAID"

"Shut up girl damn, niggas only like you when your mouth is full."

I stood up, grabbed my book bag, yanked Chris by the arm and dragged him out the door, he was singing "Never trust a big butt and a smile.... That girl is poison"

The whole cafeteria was dying laughing and Layla was furious. I'm sure this wasn't quite over because I knew she was petty and vindictive, but it was crazy to see the joker get all her cards pulled.

Girl you looks good, wont you back that azz up

You'se a fine motherfucker, wont you back that azz up.

Juvenile "Back That Ass Up"

CHAPTER 23: GUERRILLA WARFARE

It was cold outside, I swear I hated any temperature below 70 and West Virginia winters weren't no joke. My black leather bomber coat kept me warm, but not warm enough to my liking. Cold temperatures affected my attitude greatly. I was really not in the mood for anybody's shenanigans on this Tuesday morning. We were all standing at the bus stop located at the mouth of the manor, waiting to take the twenty-minute ride to school. It was still dark outside, and a few faces looked like they would rather be sleep than out here with this wind and bitter cold. Of course Layla was prancing around in a sweater dress, thigh high knee boots and a thin leather jacket. Looking at her was making me cold. The thought of her bare knees gave me instant shivers. She looked over at me still obviously feeling some type of way over what transpired in lunchroom with Chris.

"Girl if you had some meat on your bones you wouldn't be over there struggling with frost bite right now. "I nodded my head at her, it was so cold outside, every time she spoke it looked like she was blowing smoke circles. I wasn't trying to catch a chest cold tongue wrestling with her, nothing she said was going to move me. She probably had been arguing with me inside her head since I walked off with Chris yesterday. I'm sure she stayed up all night thinking of things to say to me this morning, she was that kind of petty.

"Were you premature?"

What!!!!

Man I couldn't do nothing but laugh, because I had to admit as dumb as she was for that it was funny.

"You know how those babies be with the big heads and little bodies."

Oh yeah she was being cutthroat because my uncle's girlfriend just had a baby that was born premature, because a few girls jumped her in the hallway on Male Court.

Before I could speak up Kallie who was still on tip from her soap opera episode went beast mode.

"Muthafuckas in glass houses shouldn't throw stones! Yo aren't you an expert on people with developmental issues, aren't you a helpers aid in the special needs classes. Every time I walk to the other end of the hallway. You in that one class, is that we why never see you but at lunch?"

Everybody was trying to pick their mouth off the floor. I never saw a lot of my friends because I was in honor classes but I didn't know she was in the learning disability room.

Layla's face was even shocked; her secret was out.

Kaylie didn't stop, "Your nasty attitude got you in baby room or do you learn at a premature pace."

Layla was pissed, "I move at the same pace ya mama did when she left all of y'all here with ya old ass granny."

"Bitch you a crack baby though, it isn't no secret, your mama a freak hoe for that white girl, you always trying to bully other motherfuckers and down talk everybody else but you ain't shit either and your life is far from perfect. I tried to overlook it because you slow as fuck, but I'm sick of your shit hoe, just like I know you sick of Zeke and them running in out of your house get slurped down by ya mami. You gonna be just like her with ya dumb ass."

She took a breath.

But she wasn't done.

"And saying my mama ran off and left us doesn't hurt me, my grandmother been healed that pain and filled that void. We are happy and well taken care of now, no hungry nights, no sleeping on floors, no strangers invading our space, so if saying peace to my mama's foul ways meant peace to my soul then so be it. I'm content with my situation, you're the one who isn't that's why you all in everybody else's. Now come out your face again wrong and I will slice it."

The bus pulled up right on time, but Layla didn't get on it, she turned around and headed back in the direction of her building. Nobody stopped her either. Even though she was an asshole I felt sorry for her. She was paying for her mother's messed up ways. Old enough to know better but young enough not to give a fuck.

Kallie was quiet the whole bus ride; her hair was all over the place. The morning wind had her looking like the Lion King. She most certainly had turned into a beast in this jungle called life, survival of the illest and she wasn't going down without a fight. I'm sure every freckle on her cappuccino colored skin had a story. You had to respect everything that she was, she was the oldest of six girls, she woke up at four o'clock every morning to make sure their clothes were ironed and layed out for school. She kept their hair braided in the flyest designs, attended all their school functions and kept a blade under her tongue in case anybody gave them any problems. To me she was the true definition of the young and the restless. Looking at her she made me proud, I had to count my blessings because her 16-year-old life was not anything close to the usual.

She peeped me staring at her.

"Don't you start with your shit either, I know I went hard on her, I feel bad. But she been asking for it for a while, I'm over ignoring her or anybody's else's bullshit I'm checking hoes from this day forward. So save the speech about being the bigger person E."

I rolled my eyes, "I wasn't even about to say that I was going to tell you we going to the Vertigo Lounge tonight to find some boyfriends with cars I'm over riding this bus in the cold."

We both fell out laughing, she reached over patting my hand.

"So Anne Walters can roll up in there swinging her bingo bag busting us all in our shit again." Oh gosh I died thinking about the time my grandmother caught us slipping and went to work on both of us.

It was our 9th grade summer, Bobbie-O The Booster was always stealing stuff and selling it for the low. One day we were on the swings behind my grandmothers building. Kallie and I were having a contest to see who could jump out the swing the furthest. All of a sudden it's a bunch of commotion and you see Bobbie-O running into the woods with a big black trash bag, he comes out of the woods, and runs up the hill towards the circle, a few seconds later he comes back down the hill with the police following close behind him. The whole time he was running around like a chicken with his cut off he was screaming out lyrics from Public Enemy "911 Is A Joke" he almost got away but he tripped and fell. He must have thought they caught him or what, but he was rolling down the hill screaming, "Help, get these motherfuckers off of me!" It was crazy and hilarious to watch. They just waiting for him at the bottom, threw the cuffs on him and dragged him to the cruiser, he cursed them out the whole way there. You could still hear him going off as the car left out of the manor. Yanni appeared out of nowhere as usual, I didn't really talk to her as much since she dipped out when I got jumped. Of course she had a crazy idea. " I bet Bobbie had something stolen in that bag, let's go see what it was."

"It couldn't hurt he was in jail, plus it was stolen anyways. " She was looking towards the woods and of course my nosiness peaked. I looked at Kayla "let's go see what was in the bag."

We headed into the woods and it took us a good twenty minutes to locate Bobby's stash. We all looked at each other, confused as hell to open up a bag full of firecrackers.

"Yo, man he will steal anything."

We all laughed so hard, but then I got the bright Idea that we should sell them a pack for a dollar and split the money.

"Who really gonna buy firecrackers it's not the forth."

"Exactly, but everybody likes firecrackers we only get to use them on the fourth. Wouldn't you want them if you could get them every day."

That was how we started hustling firecrackers out my uncles back bedroom window. Kids from all over the manor would tap on the window with their money and we would get them together. In the first three days we made fifty dollars. Things didn't run smoothly for too long my grandmother wanted to know why all the neighborhood kids were looking for us. So we took some of the money we made off the firecrackers, bought paper cups, Kool-Aid, sugar and started selling frozen icees. To keep the heat off of us, you had to buy an icee or you couldn't by fire crackers. Every night we loaded up my grandmother's deep freezer with different flavors and sold them the next day. We were making plenty of money off both of our businesses and my grandmother was happy I was no longer in her pocket. Everything was going fine until, Zeke and his crew started beefing with a new boy who had just moved in named Tommy. Tommy was a big awkward shaped, Mr. T looking guy who thought everybody was supposed to be scared of him because he had muscles. He stepped to Zeke one day about having his music too loud, and Zeke laughed in his face. He told Zeke he would smack him like his mama should have and they began scuffling. It was over as quick as it started. But they always would fight every time that they crossed paths. One particular fight somebody threw some firecrackers to break it up, and neither side knew who was shooting so now their beef had escalated. Now every time some kids let off fireworks it was thought be a shootout, and people went running off paranoid. All the kids knew what was up but the adults were sick of the daily "shootouts"

My little cousin Hasir who lived directly across the hallway from us was like my shadow, if I moved he moved. I was ten years older than him and he was truly one of my best friends. I believe he benefitted the most off my firecracker business, I took him to the movies, swimming, the mall and skating. And he would be the one who got us caught up. He came right outside one day and threw firecrackers right off the porch in front of my grandmother and her friends. I'm sure she tried to break his neck. All the old ladies, scatter and ran for cover, a few of them fell down. Mrs. Taylor fell down the hill and sprained her ankle. My grandmother played it cool and he fell for it.

She asked him where he got the firecrackers from. He told her she needed a dollar if she wanted some. She gave him the dollar and followed him around to the back window. When we opened the window and saw him standing there with her, I think I fainted inside my body for at least ten minutes. Kallie looked like a damn ghost. We stood there in shock before we realized my grandmother was gone, before we had time to react she was in the room with us, beating us with her bingo bag. She tore us up, called us terrorist and threatened to turn us in for selling illegal fireworks without a license. My grandfather came in the room, she was out of breath and sweating. He told her to go on in the living room he would handle it. Soon as she shut the door and was out of earshot he fell out laughing.

"You girls are truly something else I pray you stay on the right track because if not the world is in trouble."

We both looked down.

"I know you girls meant well but y'all was dead wrong for using your icee business as a front for selling those fireworks. What if one of these kids would have gotten hurt? Who do you think that would have fell back on? You guys are too smart to invest time into anything that's not going to be beneficial for you on a long term basis. Those firecrackers would eventually run out but you can make icees forever. Don't ever jeopardize yourself for something short term." He stopped and starting scratching his head.

"And I thought y'all was smart until y'all let Hasir in on yalls business. Y'all know that boy can't be still. But the best part was once he came in here and saw Anne beating y'all with that bag, his face got spooked he grabbed two icees from the freezer and ran back across the hall."

He left us right in the room nursing our battered heads and backs.

A few seconds later my grandmother busted back in the room with her inhaler in one hand and a fly swatter in the other. We ran right past her and ran and jumped in the bed with my grandfather, she smacked us and him repeatedly. Her ride beeped for bingo and she went out the door, calling us baby savages and hood terrorist.

"Yall down made Elsie Taylor break her damn foot. Don't ya'll ever come outside again?"

Soon as the car pulled off Hasir appeared in the doorway looking confused, "What did y'all do"

We all laughed at him.

"Plan to leave something behind

So your name will live on, no matter what the game lives on"

Nas "Project Windows"

CHAPTER 24: DA REAL WORLD

I graduated from high school, worked all throughout the summer and finally I was settled in at West Virginia University in Morgantown. This was the first time I was away from home by myself, I was excited and scared at the same time. I didn't stay in the regular dorms because I applied late, but my scholarship allowed me to live in Summit Suites. I think they were a little bit nicer than the dorms anyways. I had a room to myself which was right up my alley. But that didn't last too long I ended up getting a roommate from small town in West Virginia. She was cool at first, then her sister started coming up more and more, next thing you know she was staying there. Her sister was so beautiful, I think she was white, but she had olive colored skin and looked exotic. But the girl was cookoo bird and a coke head. She would come in the room, in a drunken stupor in the middle of the night, crying and playing country music. I would wake up like, "turn that shit offffffffff"

She would cry even harder get up in the middle of the floor and dance.

I couldn't take it anymore. Every time she came in and played her country I would play Bone Thugs in Harmony so loud. It was a musical war zone in our suite. Somebody on our floor finally complained and we had a meeting with the residence manager. My roommate said I was rude and distant. I told them I was tired of her sister's impromptu visits and musical shenanigans.

"How long has this been going on?"

"Since I got here."

"Why didn't you tell somebody."

"Snitch on her" I asked, making sure he understood that wasn't in my plans.

"I'm sure you would rather switch roommates rather than having a boom box battle going on there."

I didn't bother telling him that it didn't matter I was going home after the semester anyways. I had already contacted my Upward Bound counselor at State and I would be able to attend there in January. I don't know if I was truly homesick, or if I was tired of school period. I had stopped going to class, turned all my work in, did my assignments in advance and managed to transfer on the dean's list. I was happy to return home for the holidays knowing that I didn't have to go back. I didn't ponder on the fact that I was possibly making a big mistake returning to the same place that I was trying to escape. The crazy thing is nobody questioned my choices but my grandfather, once, maybe. Nobody pressured me to stay, so on that note I gladly walked away.

The holidays went by, and the transition back to the manor was different. I didn't feel the same about it, my room seemed smaller, the once huge housing complex seemed as if it had shrunk and at times I wondered if my brain capacity had as well. Why did I return? I couldn't answer that question, yet. I started my new semester at State and actually enjoyed it. I had to get up fairly early to catch the city bus but I didn't mind. My next goal was to purchase a vehicle before summer, so I would no longer have to deal with the morning cold anymore. My whole focus had changed to making myself more self-sufficient in my unstable environment. I think I was suffering from nest egg anxiety, I just wasn't ready to leave the nest, but I wasn't able to see the basket was breaking. The shock of my life came when my grandparents announced they had found an apartment on the west side and were moving.

I came and back and they left, the irony. Moving day for them was a game changer for me. I was an adult now who didn't have to tip toe past their porch anymore. The taste of freedom was semi contaminated.

Summer was approaching and the familiar mode of the neighborhood was resurfacing. I loved the warmer weather, as the trees and flowers of spring came alive so did I. Going to school and working back at the bookstore kept me pretty busy. I would occasionally go to basketball games, but mainly I just hung out with a few of my friends who still remained. One day I walked out of the manor to get some washing powder for my mother from the Rite Aid on Washington Street. I heard a voice calling my name and looked in the parking lot of Little page, a smaller housing complex right beside ours on the main road. There was Trey flagging me down, I rolled my eyes hoping he wasn't about to crack a slobber joke, I really wasn't in the mood. I was mad I had to walk in the first place. Secondly I hated carrying heavy stuff, because my arms were tiny and the bags would damn near cut off my circulation.

"What you want?"

"Damn, girl are you bipolar?"

"How is that a proper response?"

"You're rude for no reason," he said finally walking over to me. I almost cracked a smile but my poker face was impeccable. Trey looked even better than I remembered. He now had facial hair neatly groomed in an immaculate goatee that framed his handsome face. Fine was an understatement at this point. He was fine but he wasn't finer than Chris nobody would ever be finer than Chris.

"My bad, I'm on a mission for washing powder that I don't feel like carrying up the hill."

"I'll give you a ride."

"What you driving."

He frowned his face up at me, "You walking you can't be that bougie, to turn down a free ride."

"Man I know you I was making sure it wasn't a fiend's whip."

"Oh so you gonna keep sonnin me, like I can't get my own ride, your ass can walk E."

I shrugged my shoulders, that's what I prepared to do anyways.

He looked at me and shook his head. "You stubborn, stuck up, your ears uneven, your head is too big for your neck, you ain't even make it a semester at college and you the most important one you got me fucked up."

Dude What? I pushed him off the sidewalk into the street.

A car came out of nowhere from the Sissonville direction, my heart stopped, it barely missed him.

HONKKKKKKKKKKKKKKKKKKKKKK!!!!!!

"Get out of the street you stupid dumb niggers," the driver yelled flicking us off.

I don't know who Trey was madder at, me or the red neck driver. I smiled at him, I don't know why, he was just cute while he was angry.

"Yo you not gonna even say sorry for almost damn near getting me clipped," he barked.

"You need to learn to control your tongue, next time your mouth might put you in a situation you can't get out of."

He smirked, "is that so"

I pushed him in the street again, this time he pulled me with him. Thank goodness the road was clear, but my heart was beating fast anyway. He must have felt it.

"You gonna get in trouble, you know you're supposed to go to the store and come right back, don't speak to no strangers, and don't be in the street unless you have to," he sounded just like my grandmother.

"And look both ways!"

We both laughed hysterically in the middle of Washington street. A car whizzed by on the opposite side and I hopped right back on the sidewalk.

"I miss walking by there seeing them sitting on the porch it just don't feel right," he said, rubbing his goatee and staring back over into the projects.

"I know nothing really feels right over there anymore"

"Everybody in jail now, or off that shit, I stay out the way. I come get my money then I'm ghost."

Boooom crack Bizoooom. The sky became instantly dark and a thunderous sound interrupted our convo. I didn't have to time think as a serious downpour disrespected my freshly wrapped hair.

"Cmon" he yelled heading towards a black Lexus. He opened the door for me and I hopped in. I remembered a Bronx tale and leaned over and opened his already unlocked door.

He smiled, "I see you have manners after all."

"I got manor manners."

"I know that's right, imma give you the respect that you earn."

He pulled the car out of the parking lot and one minute we were sitting in Rite Aid parking lot. He offered to go in and get the washing powder. I was sitting in the car, enjoying the Dmx that was playing when somebody tapped on the window.

I looked up it was an older girl, with a shoulder length ponytail and dark brown eyes, staring me down. Before I could roll the window down, Trey came out of the store and told her to back up off his car. She did without any questions and he pulled off.

"Who was that?"

"Jessica Lynn"

I just stared at him, like I was supposed to know who that was. I let it go because at this point I was happy I could keep my seven dollars for the washing powder. He must have thought I cared because he started explaining.

"She used to be Zeke's girl, everybody use to want her. She was one of those spoiled girls from off the west side hill. Her parents had bought her that black Explorer with the 22 inch rims that said JaeLynn on the plate."

I still shook my head at him, I didn't know this girl, I don't think I had ever seen her a day in my life or that truck.

"Zeke thought he had winner with that one, he used to always say slick shit like y'all keep fucking with them bottom feeder bitches out the hood, and get set up. He felt like she was an upgrade because she looked good on his arm. He didn't realize until it was late that her parents spoiled her she didn't understand the meaning of no, or him not having it at the moment. She had him blowing crazy cheese on her. Then she got jealous of this chick whose apartment he was trapping out of. Went over to her house caused a big scene, the police came, found everything. The hood chick Zeke was always putting down, kept her mouth shut. That bitch Jessica told everything she knew, and made up some shit she thought she knew by putting in a call to the tip line."

"Damn, well what she doing over here now?"

"Fuck if I know, but I do know her type can't come around me. She is not to be trusted."

"To all the Laura's of the world, I feel your pain

To all the Christies in every cities and Tiffany Lanes

We all hustlers, in love with the same thang

Jay-Z "Allure"

CHAPTER 25: COMING OF AGE

Me and Trey ended up hanging out for the rest of the day. For some odd reason I could not get that girls face out of my head. For some odd reason my brain was trying to convince me that I knew her or had at least seen her before. I knew this was going to bother me until I had it figured out. Trey was a naturally funny guy, we spent most of the time clowning and talking about how much fun growing up was and how different life was now as an adult. We were both struggling on choosing where we were headed in life. I wanted to be a computer engineer at first, then totally changed my mind when I realized I would rather use the creative side of my brain. I loved writing and taking pictures, I just didn't know how far that would take me, but I did end up switching my major to communications. Trey wanted to open up a soul food restaurant.

"You can't cook man."

"Girl, my whip game official with whatever I put in the pot!"

"Everything don't go in a pot though, so your cheffin skills are limited."

"Must you have a comeback for everything?"

"Oh I know I got that comeback."

"Man, go on somewhere your crazy ass got that runaway and never look back."

"You sure came right back to pick me up today, hmmmmmmmm."

"That's because I was bored."

He looked out the window and I saw his reflection smiling exposing those pretty white teeth that made me drool all those years ago.

"Well take me home then"

He turned around and faced me, and said, "nah you hanging with me tonight. We about to have fun."

"We have two different ideas of fun," I knew how he liked to get down and it didn't appeal to me.

"Let's make a deal, tonight we have fun my way, and tomorrow I'll be boring with your lame ass."

We shook on it.

I should have known we would end up at the place I had been avoiding. Trey pulled up in the parking lot of The Vertigo Lounge. It was already packed with a variety of familiar cars but I didn't see any familiar faces standing outside. We crossed the street and I almost had the urge to turn around. Before I knew it Trey had paid the entry fee and we were inside. I didn't know what to expect because I had never been inside a club, or a bar. This was a small bar that was packed to capacity with mostly everybody on the scene in the city. Trey must have sensed my uneasiness, slipping his around my waist we made it to a section of the club, that must have been designated for our hood because that's all I saw. If you could have taken a picture when people realized who Trey was with everybody's face would be in a state of shock. Everybody dapped him up but the convo's with him were short and they hugged me, I started to feel more comfortable. I saw a few girls I was cool with made my way over to them.

Nadia was the first to run towards me, kissing me on the cheek, "boo what the hell you doing in here?"

"She fine though!" Mariah said checking me out from head to toe. I had on a white dress, that made my slim figure look curvy in all the right places. My nonexistent waist couldn't help to boost my hips. I had a habit of over accessorizing, I had on enough gold necklaces for every chick in there. Finally learning how to tame the thick full head of hair Anne Walters blessed me with, had my bob bouncing with enough body to look like an expensive wig. My hazel eyes were more on the green side today and my reflection in the mirror over top of the bar had me feeling like tonight just might be a good night after all.

"You in here Trey Diddy"

"Yeah" I said leaving it at that, Mariah was the human version of hood newspaper and I wasn't about to give her a free story. She took the hint and switched the subject.

"Look at her freak ass over there trying to end up in some hotel room for a quick come up."

I followed her gaze and saw Layla on the dance floor doing one of the nastiest slow grinds in a public place. She was all over the dude, I think every part of her body above her knees touched his. I had to admit she was putting on quite show. The red dress she had on looked like it was about to pop off of her any minute. To my shock I didn't think it was possible but the girl had gotten thicker since I saw her last. But the real shock came when I got a good look at the guy she was giving the business to on the dance floor, it was none other than Christopher Hankins. Chris, must have been invincible because tonight he sure wasn't acting scared of Layla's poison. I guess if you could grind right you could get a dude to forget about that long as you had a big butt and a smile. I had seen enough, low-key disgusted, I made my way back over to Trey.

He was engaged in a deep conversation with Arty. Arty was Aces older brother, he was one of those dudes who stayed behind the scenes at all times. Seeing him in there was unexpected. He was in the streets heavy, but he was also in college and doing well. Last year at the beginning of the school year, he bought every kid in the manor, a book bag that was filled with school supplies. When report cards came out he was waiting at the top hill of with a stack of money, he gave out ten dollars for the B honor roll and twenty bucks if you made the A honor roll. The following nine weeks he was out there in the pouring rain on report card day. He ended up giving out more money than the first time. He was so excited about all the good grades, he sent one of his homeboys to grab 30 boxes of pizza, ice cream and cake. He had somebody open the community center, and all the smart kids participated in the celebration. He didn't talk much but his actions spoke volumes.

"This ain't for her, watch her cause Plush ain't gonna want an explanation he gonna cause ruckus, plus her people give so much love I gotta make sure what she around is genuine"

"You act like you telling me something I don't know. She in good hands with me, you don't have to say no more."

I walked up as if I didn't hear any part of the conversation, and said "Y'all must have no rhythm like me over here hugging the wall."

They both laughed, Arty shook his head and walk off towards the bar.

"You got me messed up boo, my two step out cold." Stepping side to side and snapping his fingers to "Get Ya Roll On" Trey was showing off. He was in a crispy white Polo, white linen shorts and some white Jordan's. The club light had his jewelry dancing and I noticed my eyes weren't the only ones on him. A few girls in the club had focused in on the fine young man that was in front of me lip syncing. Too bad I had all his attention and someone else's.

Chris had finally noticed me, he looked at me with the same look I had plastered on my face when I saw him earlier. I saw him staring at me from the corner of my eye. I pretended as if I didn't see him, notice him, or even feel him staring at me. It's a wonder that Trey didn't feel him staring a hole through him. At that moment, the DJ, Marco Blaze, a tall lanky brown skin guy, with braids and glasses decided to get live. He got on the mic and starting talking to the crowd "It's some fine chicks in here tonight, if you got ain't scared approach one and sing her this song."

The beat dropped to my favorite sng.

"Down at the studio trying to make tracks, wifey at home all over my back!" Trey was singing all in my ear, before the second verse hit he had me in his arms acting like he made the damn song for me. Apparently it was amusing to his boys to watch because they kept asking him if he was drunk and what was he drinking.

"Yoooooooo when you start dancing with females?"

"Mind ya business in my Ray voice," he screamed over the music and everybody fell out laughing. He went to use the bathroom and I made my way back to the booth for a seat. I hadn't been sitting down for a full minute when a familiar silhouette approached the table. I'm sure mixed feelings that were inside showed on the outside because she spoke, "I come in peace."

CHAPTER 26: THE WRITINGS ON THE WALL

Yanni was standing before me, acting as if we were still the best of friends. I really only talked to her whenever she hit me up, and usually right after some bullshit occurred. She was like a dark cloud, that sucked the positivity out of you. I think her negative attitude was partially to blame. She acted as if the world owed her something, moping and complaining wasn't going to validate or justify her inadequate view of how the real world truly worked. A lot of us came from the same situation, single parent, low income homes, we grew up in a ruthless environment. The difference is we didn't make excuses we made it happen. I never understood how or why people would let someone else make them a victim. I just believed that you never lay down and take any role you weren't comfortable with, you had to fight back with all you had in you. As long as you believed in yourself who cared what anybody else thought. Learning to not let other people dictate your emotions was really the key to maintaining mental stability. I prayed that I could always keep this mindset, because Lord knows I didn't want to be out here lost. And if I ever did slip up I hope I had enough sense to find my way back to the light. Meanwhile this cloud of darkness was standing in my presence, talking about who knows what and I had tuned out every single word of it. She was looking at me waiting for an answer to what I had no clue.

"It's crazy isn't it how Chris used to be the main one dogging Layla for being smut butt and now he all on her jock?"

Here she goes fishing for drama. I was not even about to entertain this conversation, or any conversation for that matter that could potentially change my mood. I was having a great night with Trey and I was going to continue to do so.

"People change."

"Nah some people don't like to see others own their faults and flaws. So they try to downgrade their shortcomings when in reality they wish they had the courage to do it themselves. Everybody will come across that person that will make them face their demons. But not everybody is strong enough to battle themselves so they spend their life battling everybody else. That's why I never get into physical altercations with other people, I'm too busy fighting myself."

For the first time in our entire friendship, I felt like I could relate to where she was coming from. Even though I'm pretty sure she was taking a shot at me, I still felt her to no avail. It was hard to always live up to other people's expectations, trying to satisfy everybody was draining. But nobody wanted to be a failure, and letting down the people who cared for you was a different kind of heartbreak. But sometimes breaking the rules and not conforming to something just because it's expected of you could be so liberating.

I found it amusing that she said she didn't fight others, but from my recollection every time something went down she was the head instigator. She really was sick in the head, a hypochondriac hypocrite and when it came to her I was all the way hip. I was just waiting for her to stir the pot. But to my surprise she gave me a hug and said she was about to dip to holla at her when I had a free moment.

The depth of our conversation had to be processed tomorrow so I could get a better understanding of her perspective on life. Maybe that was my issue with her I never took time to get to the root of why she was so pessimistic. Before I could ponder our coded conversation any further I felt a slight tap on my right shoulder. I looked behind me to see a flustered Chris.

"So of all the places to go on a first date, you let a nigga bring you here?"

"This is a deal not a date."

"Well some shit is marked down for a reason."

"You sound concerned, I don't want you to worry about me, get back to enjoying your night." I looked over to find Layla on the dance floor doing the same provocative moves with some guy I had never seen before. Chris didn't seem the least bit bothered, he yelled out "You scared of her JayO"

The guy threw his hand up in our direction and continued to focus on what was in front of him.

"What's popping?"

Trey had returned to the booth with a bottle of water for me and I'm not sure what was in the clear cup he had. I sat the bottle of water down on the table, and caught a weird exchange of glares between the two young men. Chris gave me a hug and whispered in my ear "Don't ever drink nothing nobody bring you in the club, if you didn't go get it yourself don't fuck with it." I nodded my head getting the message loud and clear.

"I'mma leave you in this man's hands. Hit me when you get home." He nodded his head at Trey and went back to the other side of the bar. I didn't have to look his direction to know he was still staring at me.

"Lil nigga act like the two of you got something going on."

I wasn't answering that question either. If he wanted an answer he was going to have to be more specific with his questions. I had mastered the art of not volunteering information for frivolous purposes. Whatever issues these two had, I was not about to be in the middle of it. I felt a slight nudge and somebody bumped me. I turned around to see who it was and noticed it was the girl from earlier. The chick from Jessica chick from the parking lot.

"My bad lil mama," she stood behind me talking to the guy that Layla had just finished dancing with. She didn't wait for me to acknowledge her apology before she went on with her conversation. Before I turned back around I noticed on the left side of her neck she had a butterfly tattoo. I couldn't help but to think she looked like someone I knew, or I had seen her before. This moment felt like déjà vu'.

They called last call for alcohol and we made our way to the parking lot. The parking lot was live, it was hyper than the club, music was playing and people were outside of their cars mingling. Arti was standing outside of his Yukon with a pretty dark skinned girl name Tasia, from over our way. She looked super cute with jumbo box braids down to her waist. She had moved to the manor a couple of months back with her mother from Columbus, they used to live there along time but left one day out the blue. I hardly ever saw her outside, she and her mother both worked two jobs, at the Holiday Inn and at the McDonalds. They were always together so I was surprised to see her out. She waved at me, and started walking in my direction. She smiled and gosh she belonged on somebody's runway. She was pretty but she was amazing up close, the smoothest skin, topped with perfect cheek bones and almond shape eyes. Yes, she was killing.

"Long time no see; this is the last place I expected to catch up with you at. How you been?

"This is my first time here girl. I've been ok just trying to figure this school thing out."

"I want to go to school, but that's not happening anytime soon. All I do is work. My mom wants to open a soul food restaurant so we are saving up for that. I need to hit the lottery real fast. Because I'm tired of being a Jamaican." She laughed, "Your granny still goes to bingo? I'm going to have to hit her up real soon."

"Bitch you in every nigga face you can't claim nobody, get out my way."

We both looked over to the far right corner of the parking lot to see Layla and some girl arguing who was leaving with a dusty midget looking dude. We both looked at each other and fell out.

"Please tell me she aint serious, baby girl wild to be so young. I'm sure her little pocketbook on fire."

"I am not about to even go there with you."

"It's supposed to be a party here tomorrow; I think it's Kristee's party you want to come with me. I don't really have any friends here anymore, and I remember you were so cool and funny growing up we should kick it more. My life is so boring here, it's nothing like Columbus."

"I would come but me and Kristee aren't exactly friends and I don't really want to be crashing her party and then having her try and stunt on me."

"I feel you... her face instantly changed. She looked at me and said "is that Jessica Anne?"

Walking across the street in our direction, was the girl with the butterfly tattoo and brown eyes that currently was doing a number on my long term memory. Maybe Tasia could help me answer a few questions.

"I feel like I know her but I don't."

"You might have been too young, I'm three years older than you so maybe you don't remember her. She used to terrorize Jasmine. Jasmine used to steal all her boyfriends. I don't think it was intentionally, they just always ending up dating the same dudes. Jasmine would beat Jessica up and Jessica would keep coming back to stand outside her building for another round."

Aha! That was it! Jessica was the girl that Jasmine beat up when she first got pregnant with Miya. "I have been trying to figure out where I knew her from, I was outside the day Jasmine dragged her up Griffen Drive."

"Girl that day was a hot mess, Jessica talked all that shit about what she was going to do. Her brother told her don't go around there messing with Jasmine, but she is one of those chicks that really believes her own hype. She sat out there for hours, then she came back around the corner screaming, Daniel was pissed. He said I told you, then he made her leave."

So they were fighting over Daniel, I finally found out over all these years who the mystery boyfriend was.

"Daniel was big pimping back then; I remember he used to go with Ronnie's sister Alexis too."

A confused expression crossed her chocolate face. "They weren't fighting over
Daniel.

As hot as it was that night a solemn winter chill slid down my spine. I was almost scared to let the question leave my lips.

"Who were they fighting over."

My eyes rolled into the back of my head when she responded. "Jasmine's baby daddy Zeke."

"But you and me we got ties for different reasons

I respect that and right before I turned to leave."

Nelly "Dilemma

CHAPTER 27: THE TRUTH

The next morning, I woke up with a headache, Tasia had caused my brain to have an information overload. Apparently Miyah wasn't my uncles, He knew now but didn't at first. Jasmine didn't tell him until she and Zeke were both in jail. He just never bothered to mention it to the rest of the family. He knew that my Grandparents were attached to the little girl and didn't want to send her back to stay with Jasmine's schizophrenic mother. So him and his girlfriend Melanie chose to raise her. Zeke didn't care either way, he wasn't even concerned if she was really his or not, he was too busy trying to pacify Jessica until she flipped the script on him. When Jessica found out that Miyah could possibly be Zeke's she was hell bent on destroying anything that had to do with Jasmine. The result would be her both of them in jail while she was still out roaming the streets bitter, mourning the loss of her sister and her so called soulmate.

My cell phone rang and Trey's number flashed across the screen. Partially not wanting to answer, I wasn't really in the mood to hold up my end of our deal. I just wanted to stay in bed and not entertain any thoughts of this soap opera that was unfolding. But of course I needed some blanks filled in that Tasia couldn't. I answered the phone and to my relief he had to take a rain check on our plans he had some business to take care of, but he was letting me know he was on my way to bring my purse I had left in his car last night. That was odd because I didn't even realize I had left it.

I went in the bathroom, washed my face and brushed my teeth, looking in the mirror I wondered what it was like to wake up and know exactly how your life was going to go. "Get it together," I said to my reflection and headed down the stars and out the door.

"Where are you going, and what time did you get in here last night."

I just looked at my mom, and continued on out the door.

He had just pulled up in his freshly washed Lexus playing Reasonable Doubt. Apparently he washed his car and not his body, because he looked just like the last time I had seen him. He even still had the same red mark from the door on his hand.

He handed me my purse through the window and I peeped a Red Roof Inn key in console that was not there when I got out of his car last night.

I almost mentioned it, but decided it wasn't any of my business. Plus, I had a more pressing issue at hand.

"The Jessica girl that knocked on your window at Rite Aid yesterday?"

He rubbed his goatee, and asked nonchalantly, "what about her crazy ass."

"She was in the club last night and she bumped me after Chris walked off."

"And," his tone had a hint of annoyance in it.

"I was wondering if it had anything to do with the fact I was standing there with you."

Looking up in his rearview as if he expected someone to pull up, he shrugged his shoulders. "Nah she probably feels some type of way about Chris."

"Oh her and Chris got something going on?"

He looked me in my face and smirked with a look of contempt, "She hate that nigga."

"Let you tell it she hates everybody. When you seem to be the one with the issue with her?" The more he talked about the girl the more he seemed like a scorned female. Something wasn't right with his hatred for her.

"Girl, get on I'm not pressed about no broad, I'm about this money. You aint got nothing worry about she doesn't want your little boo Chris. If he knew like I knew he would stay away from her. She still got hate in her heart over her sister."

"What are you talking about who is her sister."

"Don't act like you don't know Chris was in the hallway with Juan and Marcus.

My heart dropped.

Her butterfly tattoo was for Shayla.

She bore a striking resemblance to her younger sister. That's why her face was haunting me. It must have been her that Mrs. Bernadette was speaking about the day of Shay Shay's death. Her father had to be the man in the Cadillac. It was something else missing about this situation that I couldn't put my finger on. My vibes were normally on point.

I couldn't figure out why Trey seemed so hostile towards anything that had to do with Chris. His phone went off and he had get ghost. I sat on the porch trying to process everything, but before I could even decide where to start, my phone rang again, it was Chris.

"You at home."

"yeah— "Click.

I liked his nerve. Who said I wanted to see him though. He must have called from the corner because before I could sit the phone down, he was walking up my steps. Looking halfway irritated, and still half drunk, he stared at me.

"How you end up in The Vertigo with Trey weak ass?"

"Nothing major we hung out all day yesterday, and that's where we ended up." Raising my voice but not on purpose, I guess my emotions did it on their own, "How you end up in The Vertigo Lounge dirty dancing like a hood Patrick Swayze with Layla."

"She was a distraction, you of all people know she aint my type at all."

A distraction for sure that she was.

"Why didn't you ever tell me that you were in the hallway when in all that stuff happened."
His whole body stiffened, but his face remained the same. "What you talking about."
"You know what I'm talki—"
"No I don't and you don't either," staring me in my eyes without breaking the gaze he plunked me in my forehead. "Whatever you thought you remember me telling you or you heard, did not happen could not and does not exist."
I plunked him back, "What is your problem?"
"That didn't feel good, but it's better it's that than it's something else."
We both stood silent. The weight of his words made the air thick.

"You threatening me Chris."

"Nah I'm saving you. I'm telling you that it's a price to pay sometimes for knowing too much. Sometimes it's best to not know all the details. Innocent people get caught up in the crossfire for seeing or knowing things that need to be silenced. Knowing too much can affect you, you have dreams, I have nightmares. Let it go, you feel me?

"Ok just stay away from Jessica she's Shayla's sister and she don't like you."

His whole expression changed and this time he couldn't conceal his annoyance.

"What! I'm just looking out for you!"

"Lemme guess Trey still trying to convince folks that she was the one who set up Zeke. Look all Imma say is he bogus and she solid. Stay away from clowns. It's a reason he hanging in Littlepage now we hip to him over here."

"Aigght."

"Man save that super emotional ish for somebody else, You don't know how many dudes had to check him last night for even stepping in the Vertigo with you. Stay away from bad news before you become the next headline."

"I said alright."

"Go play duck hunt or something"

"I would tell you to do the same but you move up to the real thing."

"Ok Era, that's my cue to go, because I know you hate to lose an argument or even admit when you wrong."

"What am I wrong about."

"Whatever you trying to put together in your head, is all wrong. I'm giving what I know to be true. Regardless of whether I can prove it or not. Trey do anything to get what he wants and all he wants is money. And all I want to is see my little brothers, make something of their lives. Some live this life for the glamour and some live it because it's a means to an end. I'm my own man I never wanted to be the man. Jealousy has gotten a lot of folks up outta here early. That's why I gotta defy the odds. Living this life is a gamble and I know it's a lot of folks betting against me."

That last statement of his took me back to Homecoming night. The night I was so busy drooling at Trey that I didn't even congratulate Chris on scoring all those touchdowns. *That was the same night, that*

Trey laid the money in Zeke's hand to pay for betting against Chris. Homecoming night was also the night of the murders.

It was as if he read my mind.

Zeke's voice echoed in my head. *"Run me that money I told you the kid was going to handle it on and off the field"*

"Alright look! I didn't do it. Juan was hitting all of Zeke's spots, every time he changed one, he was on it, nobody could figure it out he how kept knowing. Nobody knew it was Juan sticking em up either. Juan was ruthless, he started hanging out with Daniel, because they lived across the court from each other. They just used to blow trees together, Juan started lacing Daniels weed with crack, before you know it he had him hooked, he was blackmailing him into letting him mess with his little sister and all kinds of crazy mess. Daniel was going through it with his dad bouncing on them, he quit playing football and everything. He was really deeply depressed, so he started confided in his older sister, Jessica. He used get money from her being that she was so spoiled she always had access to cash, she didn't know he was on drugs. She just felt guilty that her dad did more for them then he did for her other brothers and sisters. So she would always come around to see them, in the midst of her visits she started going out with Zeke. Zeke fell in love with the girl real fast and he did whatever she wanted. So when she found out that Juan was getting her brother high and molesting her sister, she went to Zeke with it. Zeke asked me to handle it. But I told him after the CPS got on my moms case I couldn't risk not being around for my own brothers and sisters. He respected it. He bought it up to Trey and I just happened to be around. His whole demeanor got tense, it was sort of like he was defending Juan. He kept staying how he didn't know the girl like that, and he was taking a big risk. I could see his point but his eyes just kept dancing and he was giving off this vibe I wasn't feeling. Are you following me E?"

See this is exactly what I get. "I follow you, but is it too late for me to say I don't want to know now."

"Nah man I been holding this in for years, I just want you see if you think what I'm saying makes sense. Remember the night I came to pick up my bread for the rent, I started to tell you this story, but it was too much for you at the time. Now keep up with me."

I nodded my headed.

"The nigga vibe was all the way off, it was just like he was advocating for Juan with no facts. Then Zeke tell him it's no way around it, He hands him an envelope with a drawing of a butterfly on it, and an address to his newest spot. Shayla had taken it home and Daniel gave it to Jessica. Jessica gave it to Zeke so now he knew who was sticking up it his spots. But Trey was determined to pin it on Jessica not being trusted. Zeke told him to handle it and it wasn't up for discussion."
"Why was he taking up for Juan?"
"Why you think."
"They had to be partners, he had to be the one giving up the inside info. He was Zeke's right hand man. Any other time Trey be on tip ready to go at whoever for whatever. But this time he wasn't trying to hear it all."
I was trying to see if what he was saying made any sense. Then I was trying to compare it to my conversations with Trey yesterday. "So what makes you think Jessica is so solid. Trey said she snitched on Zeke and told everything.
"Whoever made that anonymous tip knew too much, gave too much detail. That girl was green. She didn't know all that information, before she got with Zeke she had never even been in the hood. So that caller couldn't have been her, somebody wanted to make it look like it was her. But they made her seem to smart she wasn't that hip to the game and how Zeke moved only thing she cared about concerning his business was if he had some money for her to go shopping."
Damn. He made a lot sense. And Trey did seem as if he had a vendetta against the girl.
The sun came out of nowhere and it seemed like it was right over our heads. I felt extremely hot all of sudden, and lightheaded. I knew I needed to go in the house and lay down because this was more than I expected to start my day off.
"Trey was greedy, he was making money with Zeke, and then making more taking it from it Zeke, so Juan was- his bread and butter. He didn't expect for Marcus to flip out and do him that night in the hallway. When I got to the hallway the scene was crazy, Zeke and Trey

was trying to get Marcus away from his sister. He had to call Jessica to get him to leave, everybody was still at the celebration after the game so the hood was basically empty. I left right after the game because I didn't have a sitter for Bobby and my mom had been on a mission for two days. I had left him with her next door to Juan's with Mrs. Taylor, that's why I was there to pick my brother up. Nobody paid attention to the shots because they were so used to the firecrackers."

When he mentioned firecrackers, I felt so guilty I almost puked. And I understood completely at that moment why Mrs. Taylor puked on my grandmother's porch that day when she was telling us about shooting.

"I'm going to bed, I have a damn headache," rolling my eyes. I stood up to go in the house.

"Era, stay away from dude, you know everything you need to know to now not deal with those type of characters. He don't care about nothing but money."

I knew that to be fact, because he just told me that before he pulled off with an attitude earlier. *"Girl, get on I'm not pressed about no broad, I'm about this money."*

"You don't have to worry about me, I want no part of those type of activities."

He gave me a quick hug and headed back down the steps, he left as quick as he came."

Hell no, I was not about to end up dead in somebody's hallway, I went upstairs and instead of laying down I got on my computer and signed up for summer school.

"The prettiest people do the ugliest things
For the road to riches and diamond rings"
Kanye West "All Falls Down"

CHAPTER 28: WHERE I WANNA BE

Walking up the steps to my grandparents house seemed weird, I had to walk all the way over to the west side in the baking sun to be around some genuine unconditional love. I went to place that I knew my soul would be at ease. Soon as I open the door, my grandmother was in my face, "What in tarnations were you doing in that hole in the wall last night and why is your cell phone going straight to voicemail. I have been calling you since 4 this morning. But your mama said you were sleep so I left you alone. Now you keep going in places like that and your going end up shot, or stabbed and I'm not coming to the hospital."

I kissed her on the cheek, "Hello to you too Anne Walters!"

My grandfather came in the living smiling. "Girl I heard you was in there drunk dancing on tables doing the whop and the typewriter."

"WHAT!"

"C'mon man, why are you trying to get her started, now she's about to have to take a breathing treatment because you've hyped her all the way up."

"Why were you drinking whiskey, and I gave you my last twenty dollars for school." He was always somewhere instigating. Now I'm sure if she had a breathalyzer she would have administered it.

"You better be careful, you're grandfather used to be a drunk!" she screamed.

His expression was beyond priceless. His eyes almost burst out of his head, he had the most embarrassed look on his face.

I burst out laughing, and so did my grandmother.

"Now why would you say some dumb shit like that Anne. I wasn't ever never evaaaaaaa a drunk Anne. I drank from time to time Anne, but a drunk I was not Anne. Ever since I could remember I haven't had time to drink, I was always working two jobs, and making sure these kids and everybody else's was straight. If anything I deserved a drink now."

She leaned close to me, on the couch and said, "he was a drunk."

We both fell out on the couch laughing and he just shook his head at my grandmother, "Girl you oughta quit."

I kicked my shoes off and stretched out on the couch with my head in my grandmother's lap. She ran her fingers through my hair, and massaged my scalp.

"Who told ya'll I was at the Vertigo Lounge last night."

"A little birdy flew in my ear." She really killed me with that line.

"Grandaddy who all been over here today?"

"Chris stopped by earlier today to bring me some medicine and he was huffing and puffing about you being in the---"

"Johnnnnnnnnnnnnnnnnnnnnnnnnnnnnnnnn!"

"Hahahhahahh" I laughed knowing my grandfather was going to tell it all. My grandmother threw the remote at him, "Now you know that boy made you promise not tell her he told you." She threw the VCR remote at him to "And you just can't hold water, even if it's the spit in your mouth."

He just smiled. "I never said nothing about him telling us anything. YOU just did." He winked at me and she sat there speechless. Then she popped me on the forehead, "You not slick."

The phone rang, my grandfather answered, I could tell by the way he was shaking his head that it was Miyah. "Girl C'mon"

"She just left, she went home for one day and she coming back? What's her excuse now."

He burst out laughing, and could barely get it out, "She said her daddy is on the couch snoring and she can't concentrate with her lego blocks. Then she said he tried to poison her, he wont let her add sugar to her Koolaid, because he thinks it's makes kids hyper. And every time she drinks some her blood pressure goes up."

My grandmother rolled her eyes. "You know I think Miya might be worse than you child. I didn't think that was possible but she will go home and call back over here every hour, asking do we want her to come back."

I laughed, remembering how I couldn't get enough of my grandparent's house. They made my childhood memorable, they were the funniest, sweetest, motivational people I could ever have lucked upon in this lifetime. I would never deny Miya of that and I hoped Jasmine's secret stayed hidden forever. My grandmother continued to massage my scalp. She was humming, "Before I Let You Go" By BlackStreet and before I knew it I drifted off into a blissful nap.

I was awakened by cold lips pressing against my forehead. I opened my eyes to see brown curls falling in my face and a pair of big brown eyes aligned with mine. Miya was always giving me Eskimo kisses, I taught her the trick of rubbing her eyelashes against mine when she was baby and no matter where we were she would put her face in mine.

"Princess Miya I love you."

"Era of the Universe I love you more." She layed on me, as I layed on my grandmother, and we all waited for my grandfather to finish making his famous chicken and dumplings.

While the dumplings were cooking, granddaddy came back in the living room, sat in his recliner and started to read the newspaper. Miya hopped up off the couch, and her little pink romper went diving in the chair on my grandfather. I had an instant flashback of what Miya was about to do. She had learned it from me. She took the newspaper out of his hands and started reading from an article. Her literacy skills were superb. My grandfather taught me how to read at three years old, that's why I loved books so much. He would challenge me with words all the time. Miyah would read, and ask questions if she didn't comprehend what she read, she was going to love my collection of books. In that moment I decided it was time for me turn over my childhood reads. I held on to them until I found a person worthy and I'm sure she would not only appreciate but cherish them as I had. The excitement on her face when I told her I would bring them to her tomorrow brought me joy. Her whole life I had been telling her to stay away from my books, that was the only thing we would fall out about. She would complain to my grandmother and she would just go buy Miya her own. That would suffice for a short period but not long afterwards she would be back on in my bookcase. The way I had my books organized I could tell when somebody touched one, and that would be grounds for World War.

The door opened and in walked Hasir, he leaned over the couch, kissed my grandmother and before he got to me I mushed him as usual. I would owe him forever for that beating I took over those firecrackers from that Bingo bag.

"What's up baby boy, You know you're cousin in here on punishment because she was drunk at The Vertigo Lounge last night dancing on tables, Anne just beat her with that bingo bag, again you missed it all."

Here they go. Hasir had been his hypeman for years. "Grandaddy did she take her down with it or was Era blocking and pleading as usual?"

"She knocked her out with it, she had her in her stretched. I had to go get her a warm rag for her head. That's why Anne in her rubbing her head now."

My grandmother just shook her head, they would go on for days. And before you know it the whole family would be talking about this imaginary drunken episode I had that earned me another bingo bag beating. That first one was legendary, and every time I thought about it I wanted to drop kick Hasir.

"You know Grandaddy, used to be a street drunk. They would always take him to C.A.R.E.S. for public intoxication.?"

"What!"

The room filled with laughter and my grandfather just shook his head. It was obvious he wasn't entertaining the conversation any longer."

"Anna Banana," that was his nickname for our grandmother. "Did you watch those shorts I left over here last week."

"Yes they are outside on the line in the backyard."

"Banana if somebody steal my shorts, why would you hang them out there instead of putting them in the dryer." He looked frustrated about those shorts and she looked like she didn't have an ounce of care.

"The heating element went out on the dryer and I can't get it fixed for two weeks, because I have to get my prescriptions tomorrow."

"How much is the heating element."

"Fifty dollars, and Billy Joe can put it on. He won't charge us to do it."

Hasir reached in his pocket, pulled out three twenties, but the way he did it you could tell he had more. When he looked up my grandmother landed the blow she had been waiting on all evening. "Where you get money from boy, now lie to me If you want to and I will get on this phone and call everybody over there. Now I'm gonna ask you one time WHERE YOU GET SOME MONEY FROM!"

Still rubbing the back of his head, he looked at my grandfather for support, but he had picked the paper back up like would it shield him from the current conversation that was taking place.

"I sold my old bike and my games at the Pawn shop in North Charleston."

"Gimme the phone, I'm calling down there, now whose name you did you use or who pawned them for you?"

"They are closed it's after nine. You can call tomorrow and then apologize for whacking me for no reason." He shook his head directed the conversation to my grandfather. "You making dumplings?"

"How you know, boy do you work for the FBI you can find everything out but the answers to your homework."

"Listen here you have one more time to not be able to tell me anything about this situation and heads will roll." My grandmother was about to come up off the couch on him, but he pushed her backed down by her shoulders. We all laughed because now she couldn't get back up. She called him all kind of peanut head names, before she just gave up trying to get up.

"I saw Chris earlier he told me he brought you some flour and chicken over here. So you know I already knew what time it was. I hopped on my bike and hit the pavement."

"Hand me that phone Anne, I'm gonna get on Chris about telling my business."

"Don't hand him the phone, Chris been dry snitching all day."

"Wait till I see him, giving out my grocery list that's a top secret recipe."

"Is that why you don't let anybody in the kitchen with you when you're making it Grandaddy?" Miyah asked with the most serious face.

"Yes, baby everybody all over the country wants to know what I have in that pot. Those dumplings are world famous."

We played a few games of Rummy before the food was finally finished. It was delicious and I was so full I did not plan on going home. I headed to the back bedroom and Hasir headed back to the manor.

I dozed off in a peaceful slumber, and woke up to a text message from Chris saying sorry for getting me a whipping. He just mentioned it to my grandfather and didn't think it was that serious. I chuckled, knowing Hasir couldn't wait to run with that story and tell everybody in the manor about my drunken episode. He certainly was John Walters Jr. because he couldn't hold water either.

Mind ya Business Next Time was the text message that I sent back. I got up to get something to drink from the kitchen, on my way back to the bed I peeked in my grandparents room to see them both on the edges on the bed with Miya stretch out in the middle. I walked in, picked her up and carried her in the room with me, she didn't even open her eyes once. I put my eyelid against hers, gave her an Eskimo kiss and before I knew had drifted back into lala land.

"Everybody love you girl not just me

And I know that you really care a lot for me

Wanna see you happy even if its not with me

Mase "What You Want"

CHAPTER 29: UNRESTRICTED

Summer school was going well, my grades were good and I would be joining the newspaper staff in the fall. I really didn't get too much involved in campus life, I went to class, went to library, sometimes ate in the cafeteria and then I went home. I started back working at my old job from high school. The Bookstore was a lively place and I could meet all different types of people. I enjoyed the job, there was a coffee shop in the bookstore, which is where I worked and the tips there were excellent. A lot of the patrons that passed through the store were doctors, lawyers, and upper class they didn't mind to drop nice size tips in the jar. So most nights I went home smiling. On this particular night I was walking over to the mall to meet Tasia at Chili's for dinner. We were celebrating, her and her mother had reached their goal and found place to open up their soul food restaurant. I was ecstatic, this was a major accomplishment and I was truly proud for my friend.

After ordering our appetizers and beverages, we started catching up on what had been going on in each other's lives for the past few weeks. We both had been so busy we hardly had time to see each other. I didn't get to kick it with too many of my friends during the summer between the classes and work, my time was limited.

"The building is right on Washington Street, with lots of parking space on the side. Mom ordered red booths and marble countertops, your mom is going to help her decorate. I just can't wait for it open. She deserves this, this is all she talks about is being her own boss. She's put up with a lot working and breaking her back doing these minimum wage jobs. I'm glad that's finally over. But she's proof that hard work does pay off if you're focused. I used to always wanna run the streets when I was in Columbus until I almost caught a case and nobody was there for me but my mother. All of those so called friends who swore they were ride or die and had my back they were nowhere to be found. So after that, I decided to dedicate my time to helping my mother get her dreams off

the ground. Girl I'm tired." She went outside to take a call from her
uncle and I pulled my notebook out and started writing.

You gave her a voucher so her clothes are free

She didn't want those business suits so she sold them to me

What you mean I have to quit my job and then I'm eligible

*See I'm bout to protest and tell folks to go against everything you telling
em*

*You can keep that check what's 301 for a month and them stamps they
sellling em*

How you sitting behind that desk looking like you need assistance

I want to know do you have a grant for dreams I aint nobody's victim

Dont insult my intelligence

I mean, is the system designed for you to fail

Cause I know a few hard working girls that just need a little help

How about you give small business loans

Instead of furnishing all these homes

See don't nobody want your handouts I was born to standout

So save all the questions, Im do the asking

Is welfare just a joke masking

the fact that its designed to keep the poor poor

And the working class working

Hey Mrs. Welfare worker who you think you jerking

I'm just saying you investing in couches so they can sit on them

All day they aint doing sh*t on them

Wait give them phones

All these welfare queens just put them on the EBT throne

But in the mean time its a lady that has work her whole life

And can't pay for her medicine now is that right

who's side are you on

It doesn't really matter you have to go by the guidelines

If you actually work for a living

Do play the welfare game just watch from the sidelines

Cause they throwing flags on every play

And its designed to keep your on their team In every way

So I guess you don't have a grant for dreams

But what about if I have another baby

Yeah I'm up on welfare schemes......

Tasia came back in ready to eat. I told her I almost started without her. Laughing, she reached over and grabbed a nacho, but whatever she saw behind me made her miss her mouth. I turned around to see what had her attention and I almost fell out of my chair. Zeke was coming through the door with Jessica.

"How did he get out?" She whispered. I couldn't even respond because I couldn't remember how much time he received but I know he should have more than Jasmine and she had a long way to go. This was confusing to me because Trey made it seem like Zeke was through with Jessica because she was the one who got him caught up in the first place.

"I have no idea, but I've been so out of the loop lately. I couldn't even tell you. I have to call Tonika in the morning and see, you know she know."

"Facts, man I bet she know when he got out, what he had on when he walked out the doors, who picked him up, what time they left their house to get him, what he stopped and ate, who he called on the way back. Matter of fact call her when we leave here. Tell her we on the way to meet us on the court."

"I wanna go say hi, he was cool as hell growing up, but I don't like the Jasmine situation especially if he really home and she isn't......... and if Miya is really his."

Tasia gave me a sympathetic look.

I didn't even want to think about how this could affect that precious little girl. She was so content and happy these days I would hate for anything to shake up her world. My grandparents had the slightest clue that she wasn't their granddaughter. Maybe he would just move out of town, and disappear.   We didn't have much time to discuss Zeke because he was standing at our table. He looked exactly the same, same jet black skin, with jet black waves only difference was the fact that he was buff as hell. Chest was cockier than when he left and his shirt was quite snug exposing muscle for days. Jessica was nowhere in sight and I wondered where she had dipped off too.

"Hey arent' you Mr. Joe's granddaughter. Damn, it's been awhile, I havent' seen you since you were on the field for Homecoming."

When he mentioned Homecoming, my body went numb. For some

reason I felt as if he mentioned it on purpose to see how good my recollection of it was. I kept my poker face and just smiled.

He continued, "You got a number for your grandparent's? That was one of the first places I hit up when I got home, I was crushed to see they had moved they were like the heart of the hood."

"Give me your number I'll have my granddaddy call you, I'm on my way there when I leave here" I said. Not wanting him to contact them before I did.

He reached into his pocket and pulled out a knot of hundreds, he pressed it in my palm. "Give this to Mrs. Anne for the little girl, you ain't gotta mention where it came from to nobody. Just say one of Jasmine's people looked out for her daughter."

I understood why Jessica wasn't around. He didn't want her to hear that part of the conversation. The part that confirmed that Miya was his or at least could be. Or maybe he was just looking out like he said, but I seriously doubted it. Me and Tasia exchange glances, and suddenly Jessica popped up with a

Carry Out bag and a drink carrier. She had on a tan floor maxi length dress, and her shoulder length hair was curled all over her head. She didn't have any make up on and her natural skin was glowing. The butterfly tattoo was drawing my attention, she paused when she saw me staring at it.

"Nice tattoo," I said. I don't know what made me do it. But I reached in my bag, pulled out my notebook and showed her the picture similar to her tattoo that was drawn in there years ago. She rubbed the page, and closed her eyes. I don't know if she was fighting back tears or reminiscing. But when she opened them, she spoke softly.

"Shayla was my sister, she always drew pictures of butterflies and gave them to me. This is one of her actual drawings." She stopped and it seemed as if she drifted off into a deep memory, rubbing her tattoo, she asked softly "You're the girl that was going to buy her ice cream, when she disappeared that day, right?"

"Yes"

I guess that was enough to make her feel comfortable enough to get whatever she needed off her chest. She sat the food on the booth behind us and sat down beside me at the table. Rubbing her hands together in a whispered tone she asked, "Why were you in the car with Trey, the other day?"

"I was actually walking to Rite Aid, I stopped and talked to him on the way, it started raining he gave me a ride. Then invited me out, we ended up at The Verigo that was the first and last time we ever hung out." I paused. "Why did you tap on the window that day? What were you going to say?"

She looked at me, "You looked out for my sister that day, I was going to look out for you. That's why I bumped you in the club. I was trying to get your attention to warn you that he's not good peeps. But my homie said somebody already got the word to you so I left it alone. I get these vibes and mine has always been off with him. I keep trying to tell Zeke, but he's hard headed and stuck on this day one homie shit. But I see through the bull. That boy has drug my name through the mud with no facts."

Running her hands through her hair she peered out the window and spoke in fed up tone. "As soon as I piece this puzzle together I'm going to make him pay." Her eyes told a story that showed she was still feeling guilty about whatever transpired that day. I found it odd that Trey said she was out to get Chris when in reality she was out to get him. I remembered Chris's advice and took it, sometimes not knowing is better and from this point on I was playing dumb.

She thanked me for her being nice to her sister, Zeke left some money to cover our meal and he dipped out of the restaurant with Jessica on his arm. Her turned around and nodded his head at me. I guess to remind me not to mention the money he just dropped for the little girl I'm sure was stretched out in my grandparents bed.

CHAPTER 30: WHEN THE SMOKE CLEARS

It was a warm July night, the sky was clear with stars illuminating the sidewalks of the City of Charleston, we walked over to the transit mall to wait for a bus that would carry us back home. The bus ride was short and before long we were walking back into the place we called The Woo. Tasia still wanted to know why Zeke was out and Crystal wasn't so we went to the Court and started throwing rocks at Tonika's window. We both had cell phones, but this was a tradition, so we lit her window up. She came to the window cursing and we both laughed. "Get down here" Tasia yelled.

"What's yall's damn problem, both of you ran out of minutes at the same time or something because if that's the case a knock or the door works just fine."

"Girl shut up and get down here."

A few moments later, Tonika was sliding down the steps in a blue jean jumper and her hair pulled back in a tight ponytail. Her Reebok Classics were sparkling white, and she was trying her hardest not to get a stain on them coming down the dingy hallway stairs.

"What is so important that all this is necessary.?"

"Zeke is out, how and why?"

"OOOOhh! He won his appeal, Something about them not being able to tie it him, and because Jasmine wouldn't talk he can't be charged. They found out it wasn't Jessica that made the call, a fiend came forth and said she was paid to make that call. Nobody has seen her since but she wouldn't tell who paid her just that it wasn't Jessica and she felt bad, because she learned that the person was a bad person."

"Man how do you be knowing this stuff." Tasia asked the question that was on my mind.

"I heard him when he was telling my cousin Joe, then I asked him was Jasmine getting out and he said he was working on it."

"You just interrupted their conversation and asked that man that?"

"Hell he interrupted mine I was trying to get twenty dollars out of Joe to go to the game and here he come, so you know they had to have a hood reunion. So I had to do a hood interview."

We all laughed. We sat outside until one in the morning cracking jokes and catching up, and of course she had all the juice. She looked at me and said "Oh you not gonna tell us about your drunken night at the Vertigo Lounge. Yes! I heard! I sent you a message on Myspace too. I know you saw it."

"Girl shut up I don't even check my myspace like that, and that is not true. My grandfather made that rumor up messing with my grandmother and Hasir ran with it. I can't believe it made it all the way back over here. I'm punching Hasir when I see him."

"You know you were drunk, it's ok nun's slip up."

"Please tell her I was not drunk, Tasia."

"She wasn't drunk she was too busy couple skating on the dance floor with Trey Diddy."

" Yeah I heard about that too, but you know he out here reckless don't nobody really deal with him no more, everybody saying he be on some snake shit behind money. He been hanging in Littlepage now."

"I haven't heard from him since that day, I left my purse in his car and he brought it, caught a little attitude and I blocked his number."

"Yeah he something else, Ya'll wouldn't have worked anyways he has a nasty attitude and your mouth is too smart. Plush would have been cracking his skull every single day."

We heard some talking coming from the back side of the building and a few seconds later. Mrs. Gracie appeared carrying a large television in her arms. She didn't pay us any attention, and kept right on trucking past us on up the court.

I reached in my purse to get my phone out to call Chris and let him know what his mother was up to. He answered on the third ring, sound extremely groggy, "Yo E, you good, what's wrong?"

"Your mom is coming up the court with a television, I don't know where she headed to but she is moving fast." I see where Chris got his speed from.

I forgot how fast Chris was because he came flying around the corner while I still had the phone up to my ear. He caught her before she hit the buildings edge and snatched the television from her. Went through her pockets and took some keys. He looked at her in disgust, "That was your third strike baby. You now belong to the hood. I got all the love for you in the world. But it's just from a distance at this point. When you get yourself all the way together you can come back. I'm 19 now I can get custody of my brothers."

"Give me five dollars and I'll be out of your way."

He turned his back on the woman who brought him into this world and cut across the other side of the court back in the darkness. She didn't yell out for her son, or offer to get her life on track for the sake of the other four she had at home. Instead she called him "an ungrateful motherfucker" and continued on her mission empty handed.

I looked at Tasia, who's eye were filled with tears.

"Why is your ass about to cry, you act like you was gonna cop the television off of her or something." Tonika reached over and patted her arm, "like for real what's up?"

"When we left here the first time my mom was chasing a guy from Columbus that used to come down here to make his money. We up and left everything we knew here because he sold her a dream. When we got there he didn't have the nice big house he promised, he had rinky dinky apartment on this horrible street that he shared with some mean old lady. She was hardly there so she didn't mind him staying but she made it clear that we couldn't stay there long. She would do all kinds of petty stuff like hide all the dishes so we couldn't eat, make us sit in the dark after 8 so we wouldn't run up her electricity. It was just crazy. But my mom wasn't for it, she found us a place after a week. It was a nice townhouse in a quiet neighborhood, she found her a good job in a law firm and It seemed like things were going well. Come to find out he didn't really stay with that woman, she was a family member and he had a whole family on the other side of town. When my mom found out she was livid. She lost it for a minute and started hanging out in bars, lost her job and I thought she was on drugs for minute because she was always pawning our stuff. I was so happy when she finally snapped out of it and said she was moving back here. She called your grandmother, and conversation about some chicken and dumplings made her want to move back and open a restaurant. I was so happy to help her see her dream through I got an extra job to speed up the process. I just get emotional when I see how easy it to almost lose focus and hope, but it takes real strength from within to overcome it. I almost caught a case in Columbus I hit a girl who was bullying me with a rock and her people pressed charges. My mom was the only one who stood by me the whole time. The friends I had made up there were scared of the girl so they stopped dealing with me period. I'm just happy to be back here even if it's not the ideal situation, I at least know I am in charge of my destiny and I'll be alright long as I keep my eyes on the prize."

Beep.

I looked down at my phone a text message had come through from Chris.

Come over here. I hugged my homegirls, told Tasia I was proud of her and headed over to the next court to Chris's. I tapped softly on the door "It's open" he yelled from inside. He was sitting in the living room on nice sectional with his feet propped up on the glass table. I hadn't been inside his apartment in years but he had done a major improvement on it. It was plush and clean and nowhere near what it used to be growing up. The walls were decorated with his awards from high school, and newspaper articles were framed as well. I'm sure it hurt him that he had to sit out from college to take care of his brothers, but that was a stand up decision to me. The fact that he wouldn't leave them was admirable.

I sat down on the couch beside him kicked my Air Maxes off, and put my feet in his lap. I had just realized that my feet were killing me from being at work and school all day. He looked down at my feet and said "You so disrespectful!"

"Will you rub my feet please?"

"No but I will pay for you to go get a pedicure tomorrow."

"What is that going to do for me right now. My feet are throbbing, it feels like my ankles are being twisted by a wrench and poked with a screwdriver."

"And the academy award goes to you for the most irrelevant scene ever."

"What do you want, I was on my way home, and here you go texting me to insult me."

"I just needed some company. Somebody to stop me from going to find my mom and letting her come back to ruin our lives some more. I just gotta let her go. Because that woman isn't my mom that's a full fledged addict with my mothers features. She got me for five hundred dollars last night and then tried to steal the television tonight. She got me so bent right now I can't let her come back. I just have to pray she comes to her senses before she ends up dead or in jail. I should have realized that when she told me she was getting her act together so I could go to college on a football scholarship and she let me throw that down the drain to cover her tracks, she didn't really care about us, the crack wouldn't let her."

He leaned back on the black leather sectional and closed his eyes. A few seconds later I saw a single tear escape his eye. That tear slowly crept down the coarse of his brown chiseled face and trailed off his chin landing in his lap. I reached over and wiped the residue of his suffering and laid my head on his shoulder.

"You will blessed, your little brothers are lucky to have you. The sacrifices you have made for them will not go unnoticed. Trust me it might not be right now but you will be greatly rewarded in life."

He didn't respond at all. I don't even know if he heard me. A few seconds later heavy breathing replaced his silence. Chris was knocked out. As tired as I was I couldn't sleep. My soul was restless, I had feeling like something was up. And I couldn't put my finger on what it is. I layed there thinking about how lucky I was to have my mother and grandparents. This place I called home, had ruined some of the best people, but it had also built some great people. I was determined to become one of the latter.

"Why we don't laugh at death, and cry at birth

Never say you cant' do it until you try it first

Be the young niggas eager to pull it

But it's a message in everything, trust me, even a bullet"

The LOX "We Gon Make It"

CHAPTER 31: THE REUNION

I must have finally dozed off, I awakened to the smell of eggs and bacon and the sound of Jay-Z pouring out of the sound system in the living. The living room was spotless and freshly vacuumed, I walked in the kitchen to see Chris rapping the word's to "Big Pimping" over the stove.

"Oh so you that's why you don't have a girlfriend, you forever macking huh?"

He jumped back and almost knocked the eggs off the stove.

"Girl, don't be creeping up on me like that. The boys know better. You almost caught a vicious right."

"You heard about what happened to BJ, don't try me boy!"

"Oh yeah, now BJ got a boyfriend!"

"Man shut up!"

The food looked so good. And I was beyond starving. "Is that your way of not answering my question."

He looked at me, opened his mouth to speak, closed it and turned back around to the stove. The kitchen was very cute, I wondered if he had decorated it himself. It was in all sunflowers. There were even real life like sunflowers on the wooden kitchen table. The whole ambiance of the room reminded me of a country setting, somewhere far removed from the heart of the projects.

"Look in the closet by the bathroom, it's new toothbrushes and wash cloths in there. Hurry up so you can make yourself useful."

"I'm a guest buddy, you wont be making any use of me this morning."

"I figured as much."

Slapping him on the back I made my way to the bathroom. Passing his little brothers room I was impressed. Their room was done in Dallas Cowboys from the rug to the curtains. I had to take a peek at Clayton and Darius, both piled up in the bottom bunk under a thick blue and white Dallas comforter. They looked so peaceful. The television was right back on the entertainment stand with the Disney Channel playing on the screen, with no signs of the attempted theft by their mother last night. A white Dell computer stand with not one but two computers separated by a printer aligned the right side of the room. But what caught my attention was the book shelf filled with children's stories, of course I had to go in at take a look. They had a really good selection that included some of my favorites. Don't ask me how but I ended up on the floor reading *The Little Indian In The Cupboard.*

"Girl I thought you had dipped out on me and here you are. I should have known you were still around being a nerd."

I closed the book, put it back where I found it and pushed past him heading to the bathroom. I grabbed the items I needed out of the fully stocked closet and shut the door behind me. The bathroom was beyond cute, Chris was damn near big brother of the year to me at this point. The whole bathroom was done in Spongebob. It was painted blue and yellow, and even smelled like kid's bubble bath. I just pictured him showering and singing Hov behind the Spongebob shower curtain and laughed. The love he had for his siblings showed in how he transformed everything he had to make sure they never knew the lengths he had to go to do it. They lived a normal life, minus their parents, but their brothers love was a true testament to family loyalty. I prayed they all made him proud and his efforts weren't in vain.

Back in the kitchen, I started pouring orange juice in little cups and putting strawberry jelly on the toast. I could feel Chris watching me. He left out a few minutes later to wake his crew up. They came flying into the kitchen to their respective spots at the table and started talking amongst themselves.

Darius, the one who favored Chris the most noticed me standing in the corner. Smiled at me shyly. "Hi Era"

"Hey you." I said smiling back.

"What's yall problem yall mouth's don't work. Let me know cause if they don't work then I don't know how yall gonna eat." Chris barked to his other brothers.

"Hey Era" they all said in unison, ranging from 5 to 14 they were all different versions of the big brother. The resemblance was amazing, you would think he spit them out himself. I wanted to see a picture of their father to see if he looked like them. I would have to ask Chris later if he had one.

Jessie, the wild one, he was 9 years old and always in to something. I used to see him jumping off construction equiptment, cars, monkey bars, anything that had height on it he was attempting it. He looked at me and said, "Did you sleep her last night, I felt you in my room looking through my stuff. And now I can't find my Nintendo 64."

Oh my goodness.

Me and Chris exchanged glances. He shook his head, knowing his mother had struck again.

Chris answered for me, at that moment I was speechless and couldn't get anything out. "Nah she got here this morning. And that Nintendo game is the least of your worries, until your tutor tell me you have mastered the art of multiplication and division aint no video games for you sir."

Jessie nodded his head and said "If I learn the math stuff real fast can I get my game back as soon as I learn it Please." His brown eyes were pleading, as if he lost his best friend.

"You sure can. I know you can do it, you're just lazy. Just put in a little more effort and you will get it. You're a smart guy you just have to discipline yourself to focus."

"Okay"

"Yall wanna go to the pool today?"

They all screamed yeah, and started eating their food really fast. Me and Chris looked at each other laughing. When they were finished, they cleaned the table up and loaded the dishwater like little proffessionals. Before Chris and I could sit down to begin to eat our or food, the kids were back in the kitchen in swimming trucks and googles.

"Go brush your teeth, wash your faces, put some lotion on and then read a book or something, because the pool doesn't open for another two hours."

"If we walk real slow, by the time we get down there it will be time for them to open the gate." Darius said while looking at the floor.

"Get outta here."

They all ran out of the kitchen laughing and pushing each other into walls.

"So you going to the pool with us or not. I will not let anybody splash you."

"I guess I could, I'll go home, shower and grab my stuff when I finish eating." I looked at him smashing his breakfast like he was eating for two. "Slow down killa, before you accidently bite the fork."

"Real funny, You know how many chicks would love to be sitting at this table watching me eat right now. I know a few that would even feed me."

"Oh I forgot you Big Pimping."

He went silent again, took a sip of orange juice, "Nah, it's just the girl that I really want deserves a lot more than I can give her right now."

"Maybe you should give her the option to make that choice."

He looked at me, nodded his head and got up from the table. He was only gone for about two minutes, before he returned with a piece of paper in his hand.

He slid it over to me, and sat at the table with his arms folded.

"Alright E."

I unfolded the noted folded into an envelope and laughed. We used to pass these all the time in elementary school, I was really surprised he remembered how to fold, the last time I tried my mind drew a blank. I opened the note to find a simple sentence, a question that I hadn't expected him to ask.

Do you want to be my girlfriend? Circle Yes or No.

I tried hard not to smile but I couldn't help it. This was so corny but it was hella cute. Did I want to be his girlfriend?

"You don't have all day E."

"I don't have a pen."

He pulled one out of his pocket and slid it over to me. Then looked up at the clock.

"Cant we date first dammmn, I don't even know if I like you."

"Girl you know folks don't date in the hood. They talk for three days then move in together. Plus you know you don't like me, you know you love me. Ain't no sense in acting like we both don't know what it is and what it's been!"

We both got quiet, "Hmmm, I will let you know by tonight."

"Ok that's fair. But I already know you just fronting to hard, you not in denial or dumb so whatever E, play that role. Now go home and get your swimsuit and stuff so we can leave by noon."

I made it to my house fifteen minutes later, only to find it empty. My mom had been working nights lately doing home health care so she usually didn't get home until noon. The house was clean and smelling good, I checked the table for any mail only to find a letter from the Red Roof Inn addressed to me. Confused I opened it up to find a bill for $578.45. According to the letter a room I rented on June 23rd was damaged and a fee for smoking was added.

I never rented a room at the Red Roof Inn.

I called the number at the bottom of the letter and asked to speak to the manager.

"Kelly Dawson speaking."

"Hello I am calling in reference to a bill received concerning a rent that I did no rent on June 23rd. I have not ever rented a room there, nor a room period. I am only 18 years old and I'm confused as to how I'm being billed for this."

"Can you give me the reference number and the last name on the letter."

"Walters, 00006081989"

After checking the information, she informed me that I checked in to the hotel at 4:15 am with my identification and didn't bother to check out. When the room was clean, cigarettes were left all over the room as long as marijuana residue and cigar wrappings. A lamp was also broken, and the iron was missing.

"Ma'm I'm sorry but I have never been to your hotel. Do you have surveillance of the front desk, if so can I please watch it to see who is using my name?"

"Yes I do and you can come in and see a copy of the ID they used to check in as well. Come in any time tomorrow after one and I will have the information available for you."

"Thank you, I shall see you tomorrow." Hanging up the phone I was puzzled as ever. This had to be some kind of mix up. I opened my purse to find my ID and to my surprise there was a wad of money. It took me a second to realize that Zeke had given me the money last night and I had forgotten to give it to my grandparents. I opened my wallet to get my ID out, It was right in the wallet and I couldn't figure out how someone had rented a room with my ID and I had it. Unless some had a fake ID with my name on it. I couldn't wait until tomorrow to see who had me twisted.

"Starting today and tomorrow's the new

And I'm still loco enough

To choke you to death with a Charleston Chew"

Dr. Dre featuring Eminem "Still Dre"

CHAPTER 32: THE LAST OF A DYING BREED

After I was showered, oiled up and dressed for the pool, I headed down the street back to Chris's house. Halfway down there I saw Hasir, he was riding a bicycle across the top of the court. When he spotted me he did a u-turn, turning up so much dust in the process when he arrived in front of me he began coughing terribly.

"What are you doing boy, you better not be causing any trouble."

"I'm not Im bored as ever tho."

"I'm about to go to the pool with Chris and his brothers your homie Quantez going you wanna-"

"I'm going I'll be back in ten minutes I have to go get my stuff."

I couldn't help but chuckle, I could have said I was going to eat fried rats on the moon and he was coming. When it came to me and my desitinations he never waited to be invited he just always tagged along like the shadow that wouldn't leave. I watched him paddle full blast back down the street, his oversized 76ers jersey blowing in the wind. I loved Iverson, so did he. We would often sit up with Grandaddy and watch his games. I loved the ruggedness that exuded from that dude, his Virginia demeanor was definitely worthy of all my attention.

In the midst of daydreaming about Allen Iverson, a car horn beeped and I looked over to see my uncle Plush's girlfriend Amina.

"Where you going girly."

She was a pretty girl, who minded her own business and never really hung outside too much. If you didn't see her coming and going to work you would forget she even lived in the manor.

"Hey Mina Mina! Can you please do me a big favor. I have to get to

179

the west side to my grandparent's right fast can you run me over there and back here"

"Yes it has to be fast though I have to go to work at 1:30."

"Oh it won't be nowhere near that long at all."

"Hop In." She turned her stereo system back up blasting Eve's "Gotta Man" all through the west side. Her driving was terrible. She was flying up side streets, slamming on breaks at stop signs all while rapping the lyrics really loud. The doobie wrap on her head was flying in every which direction, she was nodding her head so hard I wasn't sure how she could even concentrate on the road. Mina's nails were manicured to perfection with French tips, her middle finger was swinging from side to side out the window. Her cell phone rang and she immediately turn the music down, and answered the phone in the most professional voice ever. If I hadn't been in the car with her I would have sworn I was listening to a middle aged white woman.

"Amina Jefferson speaking."

She rolled her eyes. "Yes, I can reschedule your appointment to next Monday if that would better accommodate your needs. I already have your information so all you would need to do is call back Friday before close of business to confirm................ Yes thank you... Have a great day."

Soon as she hit the end button she turned her music back up and turned into the female DMX barking along to "What These Bitches Want."

I don't know what I just witnessed but it was hilarious. Her phone kept ringng and she kept answering calls switching from Martha Stewart to Lil Kim every time.

When we arrived at my grandmother's she was on a call so she stayed in the car. I ran up the sidewalk anxious to bless Joe and Anne

Walters with the money I knew would help them out. I walked through the door and they were both sitting in the floor playing Monopoly with Miya. When I walked in the girls looked at me and my grandfather swiped from the money from the bank. I laughed inwardly, this man just had to cheat, he was going to win regardless.

Miya hopped up, ran over to me and gave me an Eskimo kiss. She looked so pretty today her hair was braided up in a ponytail with purple beads hanging down. She had on a purple tie dyed short set, and her purple and white converse sneakers set her fit off nicely. My grandmother had on a blue jean dress and some flat white sandals, her hair was curled really pretty, I reached in my purse to get my camera out so I could capture the beauty they both possessed.

Before I could get my camera a weird sensation went through my whole body. I closed my eyes feeling as if I was going to faint. I shook it off but I still felt weird. My chest was hurting for some odd reason. Maybe I shouldn't go to the pool.

"E do you have any money I wanted to take Miya to the movies but the bank account is overdrawn."

"I'm fine Nanna Monopoly is fun plus I'm winning."

"Actually I do have some money for you, but its not from me." Both of them had confused faces, "Miya go get some ice cream."

Once she was out of sight I said, "here is some money from a friend that said thanks for looking out for Miya" I reached in my purse and handed over the wad of money to my grandmother. She looked at my grandfather, who said "Girl count it."

She counted out $2500 and I have never seen her move so fast in her life. She went from the living room to the bedroom, had her hat on and big purse before I even had mine closed.

Miya was on her way out of the kitchen, my grandmother had her out the door and down the steps, before I even got the chance to tell my grandfather bye. I kissed him on the forehead and headed down behind my female family members.

"Hey Mrs. A."

"Hello Amina, are you off today baby."

" No, I just gave Era a ride over here, do you need a ride somewhere? I can take you if it's not far."

"Hell no, last time I rode with you I almost had a stroke, My earrings flew out the window and all that loud rapping you do is not good for my nerves. Thank you Amina but they don't make enough seat belts to make me feel safe with your driving. Era can take that risk if she want to but me and this baby here aint about to do it honey" She waved us off and pulled Miya, in the direction of the bus stop.

Amina just smiled. The way home was a lot smoother ride considering she was on a conference call the whole way back. Soon as we pulled up to the manor. My phone was ringing it. It was Chris.

"I just got back in the manor. I'm on my way to your crib don't be rushing me boy."

"Nah E, you haven't heard."

"Heard what."

"Never mind I see you." He walked over to the car looking like he had just seen a ghost.

ERRRRRRRRRRRREEEHHHHHHHHHH ERRRRRRRRRRRRRREEEEEEEEEH

Police cars whizzed by us flying up the hill. Amina nodded me off, blew me kiss and I got out of her car to see what had Chris freaked out.

"My bad we can go now, I had to run over to my Grandparent's house. I'm just waiting on Hasir to come back down the hill he's going with us."

He opened his mouth, and nothing came out.

My phone rang, it was Plush.

"Hey uncle." I figured my grandmother told him that I was riding with Amina and he was making sure I was safe. Now I understood why he never rode with her.

"Where are you?"

" on Male Court with Chris, waiting on Hasir's slow butt so we can go to the Pool. I just left Nanny--?"

"Put Chris on the phone."

I handed Chris the phone. He turned his back to me as if that would stop me from hearing his response or something. He was acting so weird. I guess he was going to be funny style until I answered his question.

"I can't do it man."

He walked further away from me. Looking up the hill I noticed a crowd had begun to gather in the spot the police had flew past us too.

Chris came back and handed me the phone.

"hello"

"Hey E, I'll be over to where you are in ten minutes, go in Chris's house with him. Don't answer your phone for nobody but me."

"Man what is going on why?"

"Do what I say, you HEAR ME!" His voice cracked and with that last word. I knew that weird sensation earlier was letting me know something wasn't right.

"Alright" I said hanging up.

"Chris why you looking stupid, why is Plush spazzing, what's going on if you don't tell me now. Im about to get real pissed."

"Yo, shit wild. I'm hurt, man hurt."

"What is wrong, with you."

At this moment, the door swings open to his apartment. His little brother Quantez, the fourteen year old who was friends with Hasir, pushes past us with a face full of tears. Chris grabs him up, and Quantez starts swing on Chris, he was connecting blows to his body too. Chris was trying to block the blows and restrain him at the same time, but the boy was fighting him with a vengeance.

What the fuck is going on?

"Stop it yall," I yelled.

"Nigga let me go. Lemme go."

"Nah, Brah Im sorry, that's not for you to see."

"Why they do him like that why." He collapsed in his brother's arms. His sobs were uncontrollable and I couldn't make out anything that he was saying.

He just looked up at me and said. "Era how you so calm. I thought you loved that nigga."

"Loved who?"

He looked up at me, and just put his head down in his hands.

I pushed past, Chris, and made a break for the hall door. I ran all the way up to the top of hill, I don't remember seeing nothing, hearing nothing or feeling nothing. I looked behind me to see Chris running, and Quantez not too far behind me. There was yellow tape in the middle of the street, and that bike.

Get the fuck out of here!

Life was not about to play me like this!

I was going to lose it!

I was dizzy as hell!

I saw so many faces standing around and I couldn't place a single one.

That chest pain from earlier was back with a vengeance.

I think I was about to have a heart attack. I was going to die right here too!

I felt it.

I couldn't breathe. I could hear myself in my head.

I was going deaf. I couldn't hear anything. I yelled out, and I heard myself scream.

Noooooooooooooooooooooooooooooooooooooooooooo!

I knew who it was, I felt who it was. I didn't need to see the Jersey to understand how fucked up life was at this point. I dropped on my knees in front this whole crowd and did what my Grandmother Dora taught me do.

Dear Lord,

This has to be a dream, please don't let this be a reality. This is a baby. This has to be a mistake because this cannot be real. I am thanking you in advance because I know you are going to fix this. I know you are real and he is not dead. I know Jesus loves the little children. I am calling on you Heavenly Father to please let this not be.

I stayed on my knees with my eyes closed, praying and pleading. I heard Plushes voice, then Vina's. I heard Quantez screaming, I heard little boys going off. I refused to open my eyes until it was fixed.

Prayers heals.

Heal me now Lord!

My heart was hurt, my soul was hurt. I was going to stay down on my knees until I no longer felt this pain I could not control.

"Get up Little Lady, Get up." Plush was trying to lift me up. I jerked away.

"Leave her the fuck alone and go find out who did this shit." In the midst of tragedy Vina still didn't care about me? Vina was now cursing out the crowd. Nobody was saying shit. I heard Quantez, Lil Sammie, and Diontay, making threats.

As I walk through the valley of the shadow of death........

My phone was going crazy in my pocket. I didn't care who it was. I only wanted one call to be answered and that was one I placed to the Lord.

Plush was roughing the crowd up asking questions, everybody was stumped.

"Its broad daylight out this bitch and nobody saw nothing?"

The police were trying to calm down the scene but it was getting intense. I couldn't see it but I could feel it. It was all bad, all bad energy, my heart was cold. I stood up and opened my eyes. The coroner had come. But the crowd was determined to not let them take the body. His friends were acting up. My family was acting up. The neighborhood was acting up. He didn't deserve this. The police wouldn't cover him up. Hasir was laid out in the street with a knife in his chest and his eyes looking upward at the sky.

I just stood there, waiting for this sick feeling in my stomach to disappear. Waiting to wake up from this nightmare. I needed somebody to pay for this one. I looked around to find Plush or Chris, I needed them to tell me that this was not real.

Mrs. Lucille was about to light up a cigarette. I just went over there and took it from her. I had never smoked a cigarette in my life, on occasion me and Hasir would smoke my grandfathers pipe when nobody was looking growing up.

I smoked, the cigarette, until it was all gone. Im not even sure if I did it right. I just mainly needed it to exhale. I couldn't breath. The nicotine provided a little sensation in my chest, but the numbness was still there. I heard murmurs in the crowd, somebody closed to him did this. But who?

The coroners put his body on the gurney, and I passed out in Yanni's arms.

"They never would have got killed that night it I was wit em

Seem like I coulda done mo, said mo"

T.I. "Still Aint Forgave Myself"

CHAPTER 35: GHETTO LOVE

The next seven days went by in a blur, I continued to pray that was the only that was consistent in my life at this point. Sleep wasn't even an option, there was so much family and love around, but the sad thing is I couldn't feel it. I felt as if whoever put the knife in Hasir chest put it in my back as well. My grandparent's tried to talk to me, too see where my head was at, but I just didn't feel like expressing myself to anyone. All I could do was put my thoughts down on pen and paper.

It's a hard thing to swallow that justice hasn't been served
Can't shake the feeling of standing out there on the curb
Ever since the 17th I hated July
Even though I was raised not to question why
I guess I have to take it as a blessing in disguise
See the newspapers were concerned about your curfew
But my heart was asking who had a reason to hurt you
The yellow tape at the scene of the crime
Was just an indication of dreams left behind
The night before all the promises you made to me
How I looked in your eyes and told you don't play with me
If it got too rough to come stay with me
So I feel a little guilty because I let you go
But I guess I just wanted to let you grow
Thinking back to all the times I used to fuss
I held your hand inside mines took you to the movies on the bus
Can still see you sneaking in my stuff, Inseparable us
You were my shadow and then you disappeared but our bond was still the coldest
Grew up in a moment's notice, somewhere you lost focus
But it wasn't all your fault
The life even the best of us get caught
But I can't forget all the smiles you brought
To my face, that no tears can erase

So even if they close your case
My heart will always be open
Hoping that they catch up with whoever, whenever
I'll be missing you forever
The skating ring, North Charleston pool, and happy thoughts will fill my dreams
But don't think for a minute that this is Cased Closed about Hasir Supreme

The day of the funeral had finally arrived, the number of people that came out to see my young cousin laid to rest was unreal. Walking up the steps to the church, I heard the soft melody of "I won't complain." I stopped dead in my tracks and decided I wouldn't complain either. I would just remember every good time we shared. I let everyone else go in the church and I crept off to a bench on the side. The sun was shining bright, it was a beautiful day, with a clear blue sky. I looked up to the sky and dared a tear to fall. I needed good memories to soothe my heart at this moment, because I would not keep one of him lying in a

casket with me. I sat there and thought about all the times at the swimming pool, the movie theaters, the skating rings, how his smile was just one of kind. I thought of all the trouble he would unknowingly get me in, and how his smile could manage to erase whatever irritation I had with him out of my mind. I close my eyes and that's all I could picture. I felt a tear trying to slide down, but I forced myself to suck it up, to remember that smile. Before I knew it I ended up looking up at the sky and smiling myself.

Damn.

Cold World, this can't be life.

My happiness didn't last too long. I heard my Grandfather holler out. I heard Joe Walters yell. I felt his pain. This was real. I could only imagine what his mother was going through, her oldest child leaving this earth before she did. I heard the sound of heart's breaking inside of that church and I felt it outside. I knew men that I had never seen cry were dropping tears inside of that building for a young boy who would never get a second chance to maximize all the potential that we saw in him. I wonder what it meant it you were to look back and not see your shadow, did that mean that you ceased to exist. What was I supposed to do when I turned and he was not there? This time I didn't stop the tears that formed at the corners of my eyes from falling. I let them hit the pavement. Maybe if enough of them hit the concrete, the streets would have a little more sympathy. Maybe somebody in the sky heard my question because at the moment. A heavenly voice came booming through the microphone.

"Why should I feel discouraged, why should the shadows come...................."

Please answer that?

"Why should my heart feel lonely and long for heaven and home......."

Maybe that was the answer because this place wasn't feeling much like a home anymore. Maybe Hasir was in a better place. Maybe that smile would last permanently now. But I was so selfish in this moment, because what I wouldn't give to see it one more time. The tears fell and when I looked up Yanni was there handing me a tissue. She sat down beside me and I felt the numbness return. By the time the service was over and the funeral let out I wasn't sure of anything anymore. You could go your whole life trying hard to make it and in the blink of an eye somebody could just take it, What's the point? I don't remember anything after that. I went home and went to sleep. I didn't dream. I just closed my eyes and allowed the total darkness to capture my restlessness.

We never found out who killed Hasir, and my heart wasn't healing either. Every time somebody rode by me on bike, I felt the same pain as I did the day he took his last breath. I continued to pray for the understanding that would make me feel like myself again but it never came. Four whole weeks went by and I still could not shake the feeling that somebody close to him caught him slipping. Fifteen years of life stopped short, on a street that he had rode up and down so many times. A street that been a part of his soul, a street that had turn heartless.

I was just irritated with life and the cycle of death, Yanni came by every day she didn't say much she just would sit and listen to me vent about the heartache that I was feeling. Somehow I still managed to concentrate on my schoolwork but not too much after that.

Chris was going through it with his little brother Quantez, he was acting out terribly, he wanted to avenge his friend's death, and the more Chris tried to get through to him the more he threw Chris's lifestyle in his face and pulled away. Chris was threatening to send him away; he wasn't going to allow him to destroy the dynamics of the house he had built for the younger ones.   Who would have thought all he needed was a hug, from his mother? She came back home after disappearing for a month. She looked good, and actually went out and found a job. She told Chris, she watched Quantez from a hallway, the day Hasir was killed, and she was so embarrassed of her condition that she could not go out there and console her baby. She said she had to watch him break down, and not be able to comfort him because she was high. That was the last time she got high and vowed to never ever not be there for them again.

Her support system in the community was remarkable, all the women in the neighborhood were rooting for her and Chris. Everybody made sure she was surrounded by enough strength and love not to relapse, Chris seemed to relax a little but he still was a little leery although he didn't let her know that.

Chris was mentally one of the strongest people I knew. He was back on track with football, going to the gym conditioning to try and get on a college team somewhere. Even though he sat out to take care of his family, his talent and skill was still on the recruitment radar. I would go to the gym with him, while he worked out I would write. He would pour his soul out with sweat and strength and I would pour mine out with paper and ink. I kept my distance from the world these days because Hasir's death was a reality check on backstabbers, and he kept his distance from the world once he found out some of his so called friends were serving his mother. Most of our days were spent together, we never went a day without contact simply because we actually understood each other's hurt.

We were both walking back from North Charleston's gym when it started storming like crazy out of nowhere. I started to run because my hair was not about this life at all, but Chris held my arm.

"Don't run from the storm, embrace it, even if it's just for this once. Maybe it will wash some of this distress off of us."

"Boy if you don't let my arm go, you better save that sensitive moment for the steam room, "I said jerking away. He just picked me up in his arms, like a toddler and spun me around, until we were both soaked.

Letting me down, he said "Doesn't this feel good though."

I had to admit the warm rain, that was cascading from the sky, was soothing and calming. I lifted my arms to the sky and twirled around in the rain. Next thing you know I was doing a full fledge routine down Washington Street. Chris was following close behind me, with a crooked smile spread across his face. I grabbed his arms and made him dance with me. We did our version of ballroom dancing a big ball of thunder scared the life out of us and sent us laughing and running all the way through the manor. By the time we reached his apartment, we were drenched. His mother would not let us come in. She said we better go back to wherever we lost our minds at.

We headed up to my apartment, in what seem like a tropical thunderstorm. The heavy winds had the tree blowing leaves all over the places. The sewers were flooding, sending water up on the sidewalks and we were just walking through it like it was a bright sunny day. My house was empty as usual my mother was at work. I peeled off my clothes at the front door and ran upstairs to hop in the shower. Chris was on the front porch having a heated argument on his cell phone with somebody. By the time I washed my hair, and showered I expected for him to be off the phone which was totally not the case. It felt good to be dry and warm, so I refused to step on the porch when he waved for me to come outside. I went in the kitchen and threw the lasagna I had made earlier back in the oven. Ten minutes later Chris came in the house with the look of pure anger on his face. I didn't even want to know what was going on, and I guess that was good thing because he didn't volunteer to tell me either.

"I'm about to go get in the shower."

I scrunched my face up at him. "Uh Ok."

"I see you are already dressed and warm."

"Ok, Chris yes I am your perception is correct."

He was being extra weird.

"You could have waited on me."

I laughed. "For what?"

"We could have gotten in together."

"Get on somewhere boy," I said rolling my eyes, "hurry up I have lasagna in the oven and I want to watch The Bodyguard"

"No we watching I'm Bout it."

"We can watch both."

"Alright." He went up the steps, and stared at me the whole way until he was out of my sight. I grabbed the remote to get the movie ready in the VCR, when I noticed the mail on the table. There was a letter from Motel 6 addressed to me. The letter was similar to the one from the Red Roof Inn, except this one was crazy it was for $1246.87 in damages for a room rented two weeks ago. I grabbed the phone immediately and called the hotel. I need to go to the Red Roof in as well. The phone rang and the woman informed me that the room I rented was trashed and I was responsible to pay for the damages immediately.

I told her I never stepped foot inside of her hotel and I needed to see the video of whoever rented the room in my name. I yelled for Chris to hurry up, because this was becoming a pattern of confusion that I wanted no part of. Chris came the down stairs, looking fine as ever in a Nike Jogging Suit. I smiled simply because he was looking that handsome with his newly grown goatee. I explained to him the situation and he said he would go with me, to see who was using my name.

He didn't have his license but he did have an Impala that bought, so we took that to the Motel 6 about ten minutes away to get to the bottom of this case of stolen or mistaken identity. When we arrived at the front desk the girl working had an attitude.

She didn't greet us with a hello, how may I help you or anything. She just said in somber tone, "it's my birthday and I'm stuck at work watching the rain pour down."

Neither of us responded we both just waited for her to start acting like she was act work. That never happened. I finally asked for some assistance with my issue. Handing her the letter, I asked to see the check in information on file.

"I checked the girl in and it wasn't you for sure." She walked over to the grey cabinet. Flipped through some files, pulled one out and came over with a copy of my driver's license.

I opened up my wallet to make sure mine was still there and it was. I looked at the one on the copied paper again and noticed that it was my old expired license that I had found over my grandparents a couple of months back and stuck it my purse. I must have lost that one and it was being used.

"Let us see the tape from that night." Chris asked.

"Let me call my manager and make sure it's ok."

She went in the back office for a few minutes, and came back with a video tape. She popped it in the VCR on the desk ahead of us, after a few minutes of fast forwarding she stopped on the time in question. I leaned forward to see a familiar face checking in. Chris and I looked at each other to make sure we were both seeing the same thing.

"How the hell did she get your ID?"

"I have not been around here since high school, I have no idea, somebody had to give it to her."

"When the last time you seen her?"

"I haven't seen her since that night she was all over you in the Vertigo Lounge."

"Who all was close by you enough to get in your purse?"

"Nobody really, just Tasia and Yanni."

"Girl you and the mysterious Yanni." He said frowning.

"You acting like you don't like her."

"I don't "know" her not to like."

"She just misunderstood but she wouldn't have taken my ID."

"Ok well somebody did and you better get to finding out who

before you owe every hotel in the city."

"Hmmmmmmmmmmmmmmm Ummmmmm" the clerk said, frowning her lips up like she just heard the juiciest gossip ever. She looked back from me to him, to see if there was anymore.

"Who she come in here with."

"She came in here with an older white man, I remember that because she kept calling him Papa Snow and shaking her ass in front of the elevator. You would have thought Juvenile was playing the way she kept dropping it like it was hot."

"Ahh she tricking." Trey said laughing.

"I don't find it funny, she can trick under somebody else's name. She running around her tearing up hotel rooms, with my name. She really has lost it."

"I'll have the manager call her, I'll let her know this was not you."

"Thank you" Storming out of the motel, I wanted to find Layla and break her face.

"Im the wicked bitch of the east, you better keep the peace Ayo,

Or out come the beast"

Lil Kim "The JumpOff"

CHAPTER 36: KISS THE GAME GOODBYE

Chris had jokes the whole way home. I wanted no parts of his comedic act, I was heated. She literally had me twisted, I couldn't for the life of me think of how she had my ID in her possession. I hadn't been close to her at the Vertigo for her to even get in my purse without my knowing.

Trey.

I left my purse in Trey's car that night. When he brought the car to me, I remembered there was a Red Roof Inn room key in the console. He must have been with Layla that night.

Bingo! That had to be it, and both of them were going to pay for those rooms, because I damn sure wasn't. I told Chris my theory and he confirmed it.

"Remember the morning I was over here so early, when I called and asked were you home, I saw Trey dropping Layla off so I knew he was on some bullshit with you. I just didn't say anything because I didn't want you to think I was jealous or hating."

I wanted to smack his face. But he did have a point, so I just let it go. I wanted today to be over already. So I just headed back in the house to warm my leftover lasagna up for the second time. Chris followed me in the house silently.

He was probably scared to breathe thinking I was going to flip out on him at any moment. I really didn't care about the Trey situation that lasted a whole day, I didn't understand how always came clean after the fact, I just wished he would tell me the things I needed to know when the happened. I didn't like it that he was always keeping secrets. I brushed it off and decided after this hectic day I was going to have a peaceful night regardless.

I put The Bodyguard in and dared him to complain about my movie choice. I was going to sing along with Whitney and he was going to appreciate the sound of my voice. When he realizes that I put in my movie he huffed slightly, I looked at him and pretended to be about to cough. I chuckled inwardly knowing that he had a lot more huffing to do. As the movie progressed he actually seemed to like it, we laughed, but during the part where Rachel's nephew gets killed he pulled me closer when I became misty eyed. The movie made me think, jealousy was real and I knew down in my heart that I would never allow it to consume me to the point that I let it overpower my sense of compassion. I had finally made sense of Trey's issue. He was a jealous hearted person, I knew should have known that when he betted against Chris during the homecoming game, and that was probably the only reason he talked to me in the first place. And the way he spoke about Jessica he was probably jealous of Zeke to. I definably would be keeping my distance from him from now on. I looked over at Chris who was all into the movie and smiled, throughout this crazy life of mine he had been by my bodyguard. I reached in my purse, pulled out something I probably should have gave him a long time ago. I put the folded up note in his hand. He looked at me confused at what it was. Then a small smile spread across his face. He opens up the wrinkled and worn paper to find a note of my own. "How good is Cupid's aim?

He looked over at me not sure of the meaning of the question. I hit the pause button on the movie, and motioned for him to come up the steps to my room. He laughed every time he came into my room it was the weirdest combination of Mickey Mouse and Bone Thugs N Harmony. "Yo I know you are crazy this shit does not even go together how do you sleep in here?"

I gave him a stern look, "Please let's go there today ok. You have more important things to worry about."

He raised his eyebrows. "Like what?"

"You have to aim for my heart. I hope you can outshoot me, Then I'll answer your question."

He smiled, "oooooooh you don't want these problems. I do this for real." He picked up the gun and went first. We went head to head, round for round, it was a tie all the way through. We had agreed the best out of five rounds. It was the final round, and neither of us was letting up.

The way he was concentrating and focused on the television was sexy to me. I was truly happy to have in my life; he was one the best people a girl could have in her corner. I couldn't contain the urge I had to let him know he was truly appreciated. I leaned over as the next round was loading for him and kissed him softly on the lips. He looked at me like I was crazy in a state of shock, but that soon turned to surprise, then a smile.

"So that's how you feel."

Bzzzzzzzzzzzzzzzzzzzzzz.

We both looked at the television, he kissed me back, while still hitting every single duck in sight with his left hand.

"My aim good now that I found the perfect target."

"The answer to your question is yes!"

"So you my girl now E?"

"So you my boy now C?"

We both just stood there smiling at each other. He leaned in to kiss me, and every single moment we shared flashed before my eyes. I guess he was right I always knew what it was. His lips were soft, we just stood there kissing for what seemed like hours, and the more I tried to move away, the better his lips felt.

BOOM BOOM BOOM!

Who hell was knocking on the door like they were crazy.

Chris went over to the window and peered out the blinds. He turned around looking at me with a wild expression on his face.

"Yo it's like ten police cars out front?"

"What!"

"I don't know but they're probably gonna come through that door if you don't open it?"

"What did you do?"

He just looked at me. "It's crazy because I couldn't even tell you which skeleton has crept out of the closet. But one things for sure. Them fuckers sure know how to spoil a moment"

He steps closer to me, pulling me to him, kissing me softer than before. "I love you and that will never change. I adore everything that you are. And I'm so happy that before I go I got to make this memory with you tonight!"

"I love you to C. but maybe they at the wrong door. Think positive."

He shook his head. "Everything has a price, it's my time to pay."

"Give em an IOU." I went to look at the back of the apartment and cops were out there too.

Fuck!!!!!!!!!

Standing there looking in his eyes, I didn't see defeat or regret I saw a sense of relief. The crazy thing about this life is it can sometimes keep your back against the wall, mentally that will drain you. So any type of temporary alternatives can be a relief. It's crazy that you can spend your whole life trying to get the stability and security that some people are born with, but in the end the whole worth of your existence is limited to not being a statistic. But statistically speaking the odds are against you and you are set up to fail.

"I lasted a lot longer than most out here." He said no longer making eye contact.

"see, that's the thing, you're not supposed to assume you can only end up dead or in jail, that's programmed thinking. You were supposed to be on the field, on a division 1 team, showing out. And the fact that your mother chose to use drugs, and your father abandoned you doesn't make you any less worthy of your calling. Life got in the way of your purpose, but you, set the mold for your brothers, they now have a blueprint because all you ever showed them was the good in you. They never saw your demons.

Crazy how my first boyfriend lasted thirty-six minutes. My life was crazy. I walked down the steps to open the door with Chris following behind me. I opened the door in a daze, the police officers stepped in.

My mouth dropped open when he said….

"Era Yanni Walters you do you know the whereabouts of…………"

Coming Soon! Based On a Woo Story- Talk to Em Yanni

I'm still the same chick from 86 in the manor

on the stoop eating a banana

From the free lunch program

I wish I knew then what I knew now

That they would tear my buildings down

And all my friends wouldn't be around

I'd put my life on rewind

So I could go back just one time

To see my mama going to work give me a kiss on the cheek

In trouble because me and Lynitrah snuck to the creek

Walking past cops checking cars at the gate everyday

Head over Anne's to make up songs with Shanta

Getting markers write my name in the hall

Run around to Bowman and play kickball

Amo got me out and my back is stinging my box braids from Tammy swinging

Ebony up by the rocks and she wont stop singing

Up the steps hit the cut and wave at Vodka

On the bench memorizing Bone Thugs with Jamackau

My nanny back from Hills and she bought me a Nintendo

Me, Quisha and Linda throwing eggs through open windows

Out cold Mickey told

Put my life on pause While I'm reminiscing

Go over Mr. Walt's get Asia and head back down Griffen

Mrs. Eleanor on her porch tripping

Doing the Butterfly with Deanna she flipping

Singing En Vogue Giving him something he can feel

Misty playing with fire

Burnt down the fence by the baseball field

Cant wait tell tomorrow my mom get her check

She gonna hook me up

Cause me and Shan got 3rd place on our science project

Bev got me this walkman and I'm listening to Keith Sweat

Tarikia all loud hollering for me like I'm deaf

Foye put that pillowcase down you not Batman

Tony in his room with Spencer, Eric and Fatman

Somebody got the nerve to be playing the Gap Band

Mrs Womack sweeping the porch with her broom

Up to the circle to dancing in Yolanda's living room

Sneak to the flat top come back covered in dirt

Miss Hunter having a bake sale at the church

Shamia and Landra want to go to North Charleston to skate

They got to wait Martin come on at eight

Uh oh there go the street lights

But im getting in trouble im gonna see who Little trying to fight

And I wanna see but Shelia hollering for Me

Dominique, Gary and Francis doing something they aint got no business

Brian Jackson was the smartest with no competition

Shawnette, Faith, Candice, and Tasha practicing cheers trying to get better

Grandaddy at Rmc writing a letter

Taco having a party up Harrietta's

Lace tights, white girls, shirt tied in a knot Head to the circle

Walk up the hill, past Kelly, smile at Turtle

Next week we having a block party tell Hakeem to stay at miss Lottie Mae's

I'm going to a party and he aint following me

Next day Nanny ask me whats wrong with me

I got an attitude cant aint nobody taking me to see

Donita, Lisa, Kisa, and Tasha dancing in the Song a Ree

Making Sandwiches with goverment cheese

Jody Jones playing on the court like he in the league

A dollar for the ice cream truck and a rice krispy treat

92 degrees so the pool is free

Put my life on pause and tears I'd shed a few

If I could go back I would in my Brenda Wiley Voice

To the Woo To the Woo

ABOUT THE AUTHOR

Fiaunia Watson, was born in Charleston, WV. A former radio personality 11 years strong, she decided to go for it and pursue her writing dreams. An avid fan of hip hop music she decided to incorporate her love for music with her love for writing and poetry. She doesn't categorize herself as an author yet, just as someone with stories that deserve to be told.

Made in the USA
Las Vegas, NV
11 May 2022

48749634R10115